D1134955

BREAKAWAY

Also by Trevor Kew
in the Lorimer Sport Stories Series

Sidelined
Trading Goals

BREAKAWAY

Trevor Kew

James Lorimer & Company Ltd., Publishers
Toronto

James Lorimer & Company Ltd., Publishers acknowledges the support of the Ontario
Arts Council. We acknowledge the financial support of the Government of Canada
through the Canada Book Fund for our publishing activities. We acknowledge the
support of the Canada Council for the Arts which last year invested $20.1 million
in writing and publishing throughout Canada. We acknowledge the Government
of Ontario through the Ontario Media Development Corporation's Ontario
Book Initiative.

Cover image: iStockphoto

Library and Archives Canada Cataloguing in Publication

Kew, Trevor
    Breakaway / Trevor Kew.

(Sports stories)
Issued also in electronic format.
ISBN 978-1-55277-863-0 (bound). — ISBN 978-1-55277-862-3 (pbk.)

    I. Title. II. Series: Sports stories (Toronto, Ont.)

PS8621.E95B74 2011   jC813'.6   C2011-903534-0

James Lorimer & Company Ltd., Publishers   Distributed in the United States by:
317 Adelaide Street West, Suite 1002   Orca Book Publishers
Toronto, ON, Canada   P.O. Box 468
M5V 1P9   Custer, WA USA
www.lorimer.ca   98240-0468

Printed and bound in Canada.
Manufactured by Friesens in Altona, Manitoba, Canada in August, 2011.
Job # 67777

For my brother,
the little goalie in the big blue helmet

CONTENTS

1 Hat Tricks and Burgers 9

2 The Boy Who Hated Summer 19

3 Lost and Found 28

4 Rodrigo Davila 36

5 The Secret Stick 46

6 Sorta Like a Soccer Player 56

7 The Elite League 68

8 Using Your Head 80

9 Black Eye 91

10 Tyler's Tackle 99

11 Adam's First Game 107

12 The Boots Under the Bed 115

13   Striker   125

14   Back on the Ice   134

1 HAT TRICKS AND BURGERS

Adam Burnett glanced up at the scoreboard on the far wall of the Castlegar Arena. Its numbers and letters were lit up in bright orange and red.

Nelson 2, Castlegar 1
Period 3

In the middle of the scoreboard was a big clock. Adam watched the precious seconds tick away: 1:26, 1:25, 1:24. His heart thumped along with the clock.

This is it, he told himself. *Last chance.*

Someone whacked him hard on the back of his bulky shoulder pads.

"Burnett, get out there!" barked Coach Bradley. "C'mon, big guy! You got one goal today — go get us another!"

A teammate glided toward the Castlegar bench to make the change. Adam leaped over the boards and took his place. There was a sharp growl as his blades bit into the ice. A sudden rush of cold air burned his sweaty face.

Through an unfriendly swirl of blue Nelson jerseys, Adam saw his friend Jason Raskoff control the puck.

He banged his stick on the ice as hard as he could. "Jason," he bellowed. "Over here!"

The pass came so fast that Adam was caught with his stick on the wrong side of his body. Pivoting just in time, he let the puck hit his skate, then raced after it on a breakaway. He could hear a Nelson player close behind him, skates chopping into the ice frantically. Up ahead, the Nelson goaltender crouched, glove and blocker raised. With all that padding, he seemed twice the size of the net.

A stick slashed Adam's arm. He winced in pain, but kept pumping his legs.

His father's words filled his mind. "Don't look at the goalie," he always told him. "*Look for the gaps.*"

Just before he reached the goaltender, Adam saw what he was looking for. With a quick snap of the wrists, the puck zinged off his stick.

The goalie clenched his pads together but it was too late. The puck sailed right between his legs.

Adam spun away, raising his arms in the air. Within seconds, he was knocked flat on the ice under a pile of white jerseys.

"You're the man, Adam!"

"What a goal! Right through the five-hole!"

Adam bearhugged Jason. "Great pass, buddy!" he hollered, thumping his friend on the back.

As they skated back toward centre ice, Adam caught sight of his parents in the crowd. His mother was still on her feet, clapping her hands. His dad was pumping his fists in the air and shouting at the top of his lungs. Adam's little brother, Jonah, was waving. Adam waved back.

His father pointed at the scoreboard and then at the ice.

Adam glanced up at the scoreboard. Thirty seconds left. Adam understood the message his dad was sending. *Focus. Don't get too excited. It's only tied — you still need to win this game.*

From the faceoff, Adam hooked the puck back through his legs to Jason. Jason quickly passed to their speedy right winger, who deked past the clumsy Nelson defenceman.

Adam raced to catch up.

"I'm open!" he shouted.

Adam's teammate looked up and slipped the puck to him. Both players flew toward the net, two-on-one with the last Nelson defenceman.

Adam saw the goalie, saw the net behind him. He flexed his wrists and dipped his head, but faked the shot. The defenceman slid to block it. The goalie went down on his knees.

Adam slid a pass sideways and watched as his

teammate slapped the puck into the empty net.

Sticks and gloves were thrown everywhere. The shouts of Castlegar players filled the air. Everyone piled onto the Castlegar right winger, knocking him to the ice.

They were so excited that they almost forgot to skate back to centre ice so that the clock could tick off the last five seconds.

★★★

The changing room was full of loud music and louder cheers.

"I can't believe we're the league champs again this year!" Adam's teammate hollered into his ear and slapped him on the back. "And I can't believe you passed that one! Easiest goal of my life."

"If you'd missed that one . . ." said Adam, laughing.

Adam pushed his way past the other players to where his hockey bag was. He sat down next to his friend. "You were solid as ever back there today, Jason," he said. "And those passes — man!"

"Ah, c'mon, now," said Jason, then he raised his voice. "Hey guys, let's hear it for Adam! Two goals and one amazing assist. He really deserves that MVP medal!"

The rest of the players started chanting: "M-V-P! M-V-P!"

Adam felt the weight of the Most Valuable Player

medal around his neck. It clinked against the team's first-place medal. He waved his teammates away. "Guys, guys —"

He quickly gave up when someone turned up the music even louder and Graham, the goalie, started dancing. He was a little bit fat, so his belly jiggled along to the beat, making everyone laugh.

"What a team," said Adam. He looked around the room and grinned.

And then, suddenly, it hit him. This was the last time he would wear the white Castlegar Rebels jersey. It was the last time he'd get a pass from Jason. It was even the last time he'd see Graham's terrible belly dance.

"Hey, what's up, man?" asked Jason, nudging Adam with his knee.

"Oh, it's nothing," replied Adam, shrugging. He peeled off the last of his sweaty equipment and grabbed a towel. "We'd better get a move on and shower up. Our dads aren't exactly the most patient guys in the world."

Ten minutes later, they emerged from the changing room lugging large hockey bags. Parents were clustered in the lobby. Adam spotted his family standing with Jason's father.

"C'mon, guys, hurry up. Burgers'll be getting cold!" hollered Jason's father. He lifted his hat and scratched his bald head.

Adam laughed. Mr. Raskoff never changed. He was

always eating, always shouting at the referees, and always, always wearing ratty old baseball hats.

"Mr. Raskoff has invited us over for a post-game feast," said Adam's father. He beamed at Adam and wrapped an arm around his shoulders. "Hey, bud, what a game! You were a one-man team out there today."

"Can't believe you passed that last one, though," he added quietly. "You had that goalie beaten. Could've had a hat trick!"

Adam felt his cheeks burn red. "Aw, Dad," he replied. "I'm just glad we won."

"I thought it was an amazing pass," said Adam's mother. "Your teammate had an empty net! And hey, what about Jason's pass to Adam on the second goal?"

"Into his skates from what I saw," joked Mr. Raskoff, nudging his son. "This team's really going to miss you next year, Adam."

Adam caught his mother and father exchanging worried glances. He pretended not to notice.

★★★

"Burgers, burgers, burgers — I love burgers," sang Jonah in the back seat next to Adam. He drummed his thighs as he sang.

"You don't get any, donkey-face," said Adam. "Only real hockey players get burgers."

"Mom, Adam's teasing me!" whined his brother.

"And I'm really, really hungry."

"And don't call me donkey-face!" he hissed under his breath at Adam.

Adam grinned. His brother really did look a bit like a donkey, with his long nose, big ears, and crooked front teeth. He looked like the donkey from *Shrek*.

Their mother ignored Adam's comment. She reached back and patted Jonah on the leg. "Don't worry, honey. I'm sure Mr. Raskoff remembers how much you like burgers."

"And anyway," added their father. "You're getting to be pretty solid on defence — aren't ya, Jonah?"

Jonah went silent and stared out the window. Adam knew that his brother wanted to be a goaltender more than anything. But their father had decided he would play defence, and that was that.

And according to Dad, thought Adam, *my only job is to score goals, not to pass the puck.*

They arrived at the Raskoffs' and everyone piled out of the car. Jonah raced up the walkway in front of Adam and his parents, and knocked on the Raskoffs' front door.

"Come on in, guys!" exclaimed Mr. Raskoff, holding the door open wide. Adam and his family followed him into the living room. Jason was sitting on the couch. He caught Adam's eye and lifted the medal hanging around his neck. Adam grinned and did the same.

Moments later, everyone was at the dining-room

table, munching on burgers and salad. The adults sat at one end of the table. Adam, Jonah, and Jason sat at the other.

"So, like I said earlier," said Mr. Raskoff to Adam's father, "the Rebels are sure going to miss big Adam next year. I mean, fifty-six goals — what an incredible season!"

"It's okay," chirped Jason. "We'll beat his new team at provincials."

"Yeah, we'll see about that," said Adam, shoving his friend playfully.

"Seriously, though," continued Jason's father, "I know they play hockey down in Vancouver a bit, but aren't you worried about ice time? The quality of the players? The coaching?"

"I know what you mean," replied Adam's father, setting down his half-eaten burger. "These days, Vancouver seems so full of foreigners — Chinese and Indians and Serbians and everything else under the sun. For a while, I was worried there wouldn't even be enough real Canadians for a whole hockey league."

Adam's mother frowned. "But those people are Canadians too —" she began.

"Aw, c'mon, hon," said Adam's father. "You know I don't mean it in, like, a racist way or anything. I just mean, you know, that they do things differently. Their sports — I mean, cricket? Ping-pong? Soccer? Those just aren't real Canadian sports like the good old hockey game."

Mr. Raskoff shifted uncomfortably in his seat. "So anyway, what's the plan then — for hockey?"

"Well," said Adam's father, flashing his son a smile, "I did some research and found the Vancouver Elite League — it's really top-notch. Four of its ex-players are now in the NHL. With Adam's stats this year and a recommendation from Coach Bradley, I had no problem getting him a tryout. But it won't be like here. It's going to be hard to make this team." He sent Adam a warning look. "In those tryouts, you won't want to miss a chance to shoot."

"Well, it's good to know there's a league like that in Vancouver," said Mr. Raskoff, taking a sip of his wine.

"Yeah," said Adam's father, chuckling. "And I'm sure if Adam's playing hockey, he'll meet lots of kids just like him. I don't see our Adam dancing around in soccer cleats any time soon. Or cricket — you planning on playing any cricket down in Vancouver, Adam?"

"What's cricket?" asked Adam, and everyone laughed.

After they had eaten every last burger and gone over every play in the game, Adam and his family walked to the front room to put on their coats and boots.

"Thanks so much for dinner, guys," said Adam's father.

Jason was standing next to Adam. "Great season, man," he said, extending his right hand.

Adam grasped it firmly. "You too, bro," he said.

There was a sudden heavy feeling in his chest. Adam had known about the big move to Vancouver for more than three months. And he knew there were still two months of school and two months of summer before they'd be moving. But this was the first time it really sank in that he and Jason wouldn't ever play on the same team again.

2 THE BOY WHO HATED SUMMER

Adam rolled over in the grass and looked up at the big blue house where he and his family had lived since he was born. In one week, they would leave it behind.

Four months had flown by. Since school had ended in June, Adam, Jason, Graham, and some other guys from the team had played street hockey almost every day. They'd had some fun at the outdoor pool too. And twice, they'd gone fishing down at the river.

But in the last week or so, everyone's family seemed to have gone camping or to the lake or to somewhere else a thousand times more fun than Castlegar.

Adam yawned. He'd missed his friends at first, but now he was just bored. *Bored, bored, bored,* he thought.

He picked up the copy of *NHL Insider* lying next to him. He tried to read an article about his favourite team, the Calgary Flames, but it was too hot to do anything, even read.

He lay back in the soft grass and closed his eyes.

"Lunchtime, lazybones," called his mother from the

house. "Tuna sandwiches."

"Coming," replied Adam, dragging himself up off the grass.

In the kitchen, Jonah was drumming away on the table with his knuckles. Suddenly he announced that he had to go to the bathroom and scampered away.

"What's up with you these days, Adam?" asked his mother. She passed him a glass of orange juice. "You haven't seemed like yourself recently."

"I'm fine, Mom," he replied, taking a sip of juice. "Just bored."

"You *sure* it's not the move that's bothering you?" she asked, staring hard at him for a moment.

Adam rolled his eyes. "No, Mom," he said. "You know I hate summer. Summer's just a waste of time between hockey seasons."

"Okay, tough guy." She placed a tuna sandwich on a plate and slid it across the counter to him. Adam caught it with his left hand.

"Nice reflexes," she said, smiling.

Adam picked up a sandwich half and munched it thoughtfully. "This summer was okay, you know. But now there's no one to play street hockey with."

"You're going to miss Jason and Graham and all the rest when we move to Vancouver, aren't you?" said his mother softly.

Adam's chest felt tight for a moment. He looked down at his sandwich. "Well, yeah," he mumbled. "It's just — we're such a good team. And Dad keeps saying that the tryouts for this Elite League are gonna be really competitive. And I'm not gonna know anyone, at hockey or at school."

His mother nodded. "Well, you'll have to be patient," she said. "It will take time to get to know people and to get used to everything. For all of us."

Jonah bounded back into the room. He jumped into his chair, bodychecking his older brother.

"What you planning to do this afternoon, J-Dogg?" their mother asked her younger son.

"*J-Dogg!?*" said Adam in disbelief.

"It's his new nickname, apparently." She shrugged.

"Lame," droned Adam, rolling his eyes.

"So anyway, this afternoon — what's the plan?" she repeated.

"Video games?" mumbled Jonah through a mouthful of tuna and bread.

"I don't think so!" she replied. "You spent all of yesterday sitting there pressing buttons. It's too beautiful today to sit inside."

Adam finished his tuna sandwich and drained the last of his juice.

"I know!" exclaimed their mother. "How about you two go take some shots in the driveway?"

"You up for it, J-Donkey?" asked Adam.

Jonah finished his glass of juice and slammed it down on the table. "Okay! Can I play in goal?"

"Well, I'm not going to play in goal," said Adam.

"Sounds fine," said their mother. "But wear your helmet, Jonah."

"Aw, Mom . . ." whined Jonah. "It's hot out today. Plus I look stupid playing street hockey in a helmet."

"You'll look even worse with a bloody nose," she said. "Helmet."

Adam walked into his brother's room and returned carrying an old blue helmet with a rusty white cage. Ever since Jonah had been able to stand on two feet, he had been Adam's practice goalie. But after one especially hard wrist shot had given Jonah a bloody nose, the helmet had become mandatory.

In the garage, Adam helped Jonah buckle the straps on the back of his goalie pads. Then he grabbed his wooden hockey stick and a few tennis balls in one hand, and in the other picked up the net his father had built from plastic piping the previous summer. He carried everything out to the driveway. Jonah waddled behind him in full goalie gear, blue helmet bobbing up and down.

Adam tossed the tennis balls onto the ground. He gripped his stick and felt its weight in both hands. His thoughts rolled back to the winning goal of the tournament: that breakaway, that pass, that goal. He sighed and looked around. It just wasn't the same without his teammates.

"Are you gonna shoot or what?" called Jonah. He was crouching in front of the net, glove raised.

Adam fired a wrist shot into the corner above his brother's stick-hand shoulder.

"No fair — I wasn't ready!"

"Goalies should always be ready," said Adam. "Especially with me around."

Jonah growled like a bear and crouched again.

They took shots for a long time. It wasn't too hard for Adam to score, but he had to admit that Jonah was getting better. His brother's glove hand, especially, was getting pretty quick.

A ball whistled over the net and smacked the garage door.

"Hey! We're trying to get a good price for this house!"

Adam turned around. His father waved and smiled, then shut the car door behind him. He was wearing a white, short-sleeved shirt with a blue-striped tie. As usual, he was carrying his laptop.

"Hey guys!" he called, approaching them. "Last day of work in Castlegar, finished! Good stuff, Adam — working on that wrist shot?"

Adam nodded.

"It'd be nice to have a real goalie, though, eh?" their father joked, nudging Jonah as he walked past. Adam saw Jonah's smile disappear. Their father didn't seem to notice.

"A sniper forward and a tough defenceman," he added, smiling. "What a team!"

Adam and Jonah followed their father toward the house.

"Hey Adam — I heard the Flames made a big trade today," said his father as they walked inside. He glanced at his watch. "Let's check out *Sports Centre*. It's on in five minutes."

"Yeah!" exclaimed Adam. "Big trade?"

"Yeah, but I'm not sure which players," his father replied. "I'm just going to grab a drink from the fridge. I'll see you in a minute."

Adam weaved his way through the stacks of cardboard boxes in their living room. His family's whole lives were packed up. Only the TV, some clothes, and a few things like toothpaste and soap had escaped being boxed up.

Adam flopped onto the couch and grabbed the remote. He switched on the TV, which was already tuned to the sports channel.

Soccer.

Onscreen, a quick little man with long black hair was sprinting up the field. He slipped the ball through a defender's legs, zipped past another one, and smashed the ball into the top corner of the net.

Whoa, thought Adam.

"What *are* you watching?" said Adam's father as he stepped into the room. He sat down next to Adam, shaking his head. Adam's mother came into the room and sat down too.

"I dunno," said Adam, checking his watch. "This crap was just on." He looked at his father, who chuckled.

"They don't look too crappy to me!" said Adam's mother. She pointed at the screen just as a tall, lanky forward in a white jersey leaped high into the air. He bashed the ball with his head, sending it spinning into the goal.

"I can't believe these idiots," complained Adam's father, "always smacking the ball with their heads. Must not be very many brains left in there, eh, bud?" He nudged Adam with his elbow.

"Yeah, boneheads," said Adam, and glanced over at his father again. His dad laughed, so Adam laughed too.

"And hockey players are all geniuses?" said Adam's mother, raising an eyebrow. "Heading a ball accurately out of mid-air can't be that easy. I think soccer players have a lot of skill, actually."

"If they've got so much skill, why don't they get the ball in the net a bit more often?" replied Adam's father. "Every game's 1–0, 0–0, 1–1. Honestly, that stupid sport will never get big in Canada. Our sports here are way more exciting."

"Hmm, I'm not so sure," said Adam's mother. "I think there's something very exciting about eleven players going full-out for ninety minutes, and working together to hold on to a slim 1–0 lead."

Adam thought soccer looked a lot more exciting

than basketball or American football. At least there were goals in soccer. Basketball was just seven-foot-tall giants dropping a ball through a hoop. Football was just massive goons shoving each other around.

Of course, nothing compared to hockey.

"Look, it's finished," he said to his dad, pointing. "*Sports Centre*'s on."

"At last," said his father. "Just five minutes of soccer and I nearly fell asleep."

★★★

Later that night, Adam was brushing his teeth and overheard his parents talking in the next room. Their voices were hushed, but he could still make out the words.

"You can't be serious," his father was saying.

"Bruce, look," replied his mother, calmly but firmly. "I'm not trying to be difficult here. I just think, with moving to the big city and all — we should be encouraging them to be a bit more open-minded."

"I was only joking around," said Adam's father. "Why are you making such a big deal about this?"

Adam placed his toothbrush in its holder. He left the bathroom quietly and went back to his room. He turned out the light and got into bed, but it took him a long time to fall asleep.

His parents sometimes disagreed about little things: who would walk the dog, which restaurant they would go to, which DVD they would watch. But he had never heard them disagree like that before. It had sounded like an argument, and it was about him and Jonah.

He didn't like it. Not one bit.

3 LOST AND FOUND

"Jonah, you've got to hurry up or we're going to be late," called Adam's mother, rushing into the room. She was wearing a business suit and carrying a briefcase. "Sorry, Adam," she said. "I've got to go. I'm dropping your brother off at school on my way to work. You gonna be okay?"

"Of course," grumbled Adam. "I'm not six years old."

"I'm sorry," she said, flashing him a quick smile. "I forgot how tough you are. I'm sure you'll have a great first day."

"Hurry up, Jonah!" she called again. She rolled her eyes at Adam, then rushed out of the room.

Adam poured himself a second bowl of cornflakes. He grabbed a banana from the bowl on the counter and chopped it into the cereal.

Adam looked around thoughtfully. They had been in the new house for ten days. Sometimes it still seemed strange, like it wasn't really theirs. But in the last day or two, it had somehow started to feel like home.

Adam's father hurried into the kitchen. "Have a good one today, bud," he said, scooping his travel coffee mug up from the counter and grabbing his laptop case. "Remember, only two weeks till you're back on the ice!"

Adam's mother breezed through the room. Jonah trailed behind, making horrible faces behind her back.

"Hurry up, slowpoke," said Adam's mother, giving Jonah a nudge and handing him his backpack. She turned to Adam. "We're off, Adam. Have a great first day. And don't be late!"

She gave Adam's father a quick kiss.

"Bleccch," Jonah gagged.

"I've gotta run too, bud," said Adam's father with a quick wave. "See you tonight."

Suddenly Adam was all alone in the house. He munched his cereal slowly. When he was finished, he grabbed his backpack and headed for the front door. He stopped to put on his shoes.

First day, he thought to himself. He took a deep breath.

Outside, Adam felt the heat of the morning sun on his neck. All around, the leaves were turning red, yellow, and brown. The sky was a brilliant blue.

Adam's new school, Point Grey Secondary, was right across the street from his house. In front of the stone school buildings, there was a large playing field with soccer goals at either end.

Adam crossed the street and began walking across the field. The day before, it had been empty. Now, there were students everywhere, walking in groups. Everyone was jabbering and laughing and jostling their friends.

Everyone except Adam.

Adam thought of Jason. And Graham. He couldn't remember a time in his life when they hadn't walked to school together. He remembered the time Graham had got in trouble for throwing snowballs at a minivan. Usually that memory made him chuckle, but it didn't seem as funny today.

He entered the school through the main doors. He stood and stared blankly at the busy hallway. A group of five girls pushed past him, chattering in a language he didn't understand. He guessed it might be Chinese.

A tall older boy with dark skin and a turban on his head bumped into Adam's right shoulder.

"Watch it, kid!" he snarled at Adam, and moved on.

Adam felt dazed. He glanced down at the schedule his mother had given to him.

Homeroom. Room 309.

Great, where's that? wondered Adam. Deciding that Room 309 was probably on the third floor, he pushed his way through the crowd toward a set of stairs.

It took a few minutes to reach the third floor. But when he did, there was no Room 309. There was a 307, a 308, and then a wall.

Someone bumped into him again, knocking his

schedule out of his hands. It was all Adam could do not to take a swing at the person.

The bell rang and the hallway began to empty. Adam bent down and picked up his schedule. He looked around, unsure what to do next.

"Hey, you lost?" said a voice behind Adam. He turned around.

A boy was smiling at him with a big toothy grin. He had shoulder-length black hair and was much shorter than Adam.

"Well, not really," said Adam. He looked down at his timetable, then shook his head. "I mean, yeah, kind of."

The boy laughed and reached for the sheet of paper. "Hmm . . . yes, it's a little confusing." He had a bit of an accent, so Adam had to focus a bit to follow what he was saying. "I made the same mistake last year. Room 309's in the *next* building. You go down these stairs and out the exit to your left. It will be on the third floor of the building in front of you."

"Hey, thanks," said Adam. Another bell rang.

"No problem," said the boy, nodding. "Look, that's the second bell — I have to go."

By the time Adam reached Room 309, the hallways were empty. He pushed the door open.

"And food is absolutely forbidden in the library at all times . . ." A large man in a soccer jersey and shorts was speaking. He turned toward the door, as did every student in the classroom. "You must be Adam

Burnett," said the man. "I'm Mr. McKay. Please take a seat."

Embarrassed, Adam shuffled to the back of the classroom. He sat down and looked around. He could count the white kids in the class on one hand. There were four. Five, including him. The rest looked Chinese or Indian, as far as he could tell. One girl had one of those scarves on her head that meant — Adam was pretty sure — she was Muslim. He wasn't sure if he should know what country she was from.

Back in Castlegar, there had been one Chinese guy in his class, Jimmy Chan. Jason had once asked Jimmy why he couldn't speak Chinese.

"My dad doesn't even speak Chinese, dummy," Jimmy had told him. "Our family's been here in Castlegar longer than yours."

"...We pride ourselves on welcoming new students here ..." Mr. McKay was saying.

Adam realized that everyone in the class had turned around. And they were all staring at him. *He* was the newcomer Mr. McKay was talking about.

"... so I know you'll all help him feel at home in grade nine," added the teacher.

Home? thought Adam. *This place is like a different planet!*

"That's all for now, people," said Mr. McKay. "Have a great first day."

Adam looked at his schedule and breathed a sigh

of relief. His next class was Physical Education. PE had always been his best subject.

When Adam reached the school gymnasium, there was a large group of boys milling around the front entrance. Mr. McKay was standing by the far wall with a bag of soccer balls hoisted over one shoulder. "Let's head out onto the field," he called. "Everyone ready for some soccer?"

There were enthusiastic shouts and murmurs in reply.

Adam was surprised. Soccer had always been a joke in PE back in Castlegar. In elementary school, Adam and Jason had got into trouble for kicking three soccer balls onto the school roof.

Here, soccer was clearly no joke. Most of his classmates were bending down to pull on pairs of shiny soccer shoes. Some were wearing soccer jerseys like the ones he'd seen on *Sports Centre*.

Adam looked down at his running shoes.

"We'll be working on skills today," explained Mr. McKay. "No full games until next week."

Most of the class groaned.

"Oh, I forgot — you're all superstars already," he said mockingly. "Right, everyone find a partner and spread out. Start with short, simple passes, please." He began taking the balls out of the bag and tossing them left and right.

Everyone paired off quickly. Adam found himself standing alone.

"Hey, over here!" called someone to his left.

Adam turned. It was the same guy who had helped him find Room 309 earlier. He was juggling a soccer ball.

For a moment, Adam just stood and stared. He watched as the ball bounced up into the air again and again off the guy's feet, knees, and head. It never bounced away or touched the ground.

"How do you do that?" Adam asked.

"Do what?" he said, chipping the ball up into the air and catching it with his hands. He shrugged, then reached up with one hand to brush his mop of dark curly hair out of his eyes.

His accent must be Mexican, Adam decided. Adam had seen a movie about Mexican gangsters in the summer, so he was fairly sure he knew what Mexicans sounded like.

"Never mind," said Adam. "You need a partner?"

The soccer player dropped the ball and to Adam's surprise, caught it on top of his right foot and kicked it to Adam.

The ball bounced off Adam's shin and away. He sprinted after it. Swinging his leg awkwardly from the side, he returned the pass.

"I'm Adam," he said.

"My name is Rodrigo Davila," replied the boy. He flicked the ball neatly between his legs and passed it back again.

Mr. McKay told them to pass only with their left

feet. Adam tried and nearly fell over. He felt like a giraffe on skates. Next, they had to pass with the outsides of their feet. Adam didn't even try that one.

Rodrigo did it all without blinking.

Adam had just finished tripping over another pass when Mr. McKay spoke again.

"Try a few headers, guys," he called out.

Rodrigo chipped the ball into his hands and tossed it to Adam. Adam closed his eyes.

His face exploded in pain as the ball slammed into his nose.

Not wanting to seem like a wimp, Adam picked up the ball as fast as he could. Eyes watering, he threw the ball back to Rodrigo, who headed it right back. The ball rebounded off Adam's knee. Rodrigo scooped it up and grinned.

"I'm not trying that again," said Adam, shaking his head.

"Just keep your eyes open," said Rodrigo. "And hit it with your forehead."

"Easy for you to say," muttered Adam under his breath.

Rodrigo lobbed the ball at his face.

This time, Adam didn't close his eyes. He ducked instead.

4 RODRIGO DAVILA

The next day, Adam sat next to Rodrigo in the back of their English class.

He could already tell that English was going to be terrible. Their teacher was a short, fat man with a shiny bald head. He was lecturing them about his lazy class from the year before.

"You kids had better work harder than they did," the teacher rasped, breathing heavily. "No easy A-grades here! And that's all I'm going to say."

But that wasn't *all* he was going to say. He talked. And talked. And talked.

Adam's thoughts drifted. A smooth sheet of ice appeared before his eyes. The crisp, cold air of the Castlegar hockey arena burned his cheeks. Someone banged a stick on the boards —

He felt a tap on his shoulder. "Adam!"

"Yeah?" he said, still half-daydreaming.

"You want to work together on this project?" asked Rodrigo.

Adam leaned back a little. "Sorry, I wasn't listening," he whispered. "What project?"

"I don't know," laughed Rodrigo. "I wasn't listening either. I just heard Old Baldy up there say something about needing a partner. So do you want to work together?"

"Yeah, sure," said Adam. He wondered if Mexicans were any good at English. If they weren't, could he still get a good grade on the project?

"Excuse me," whispered Rodrigo to the girl sitting next to them. "Do you know what this project's about?"

"Yeah," she replied, blushing a little. "We're supposed to make a short PowerPoint presentation on someone we admire. Maybe a famous person. And to explain why we admire them."

"Thanks," said Rodrigo, and nodded at Adam. "Weird assignment, isn't it?"

Adam nodded, then pointed at the name written on the front of Rodrigo's notebook. "What kind of a name is that, anyway?" asked Adam. "Are you from Mexico or something?"

"Mexico?" Rodrigo's eyes widened. "No. I'm from Uruguay. My family and I moved to Canada at the end of the last school year."

Adam had never heard of Uruguay. But he didn't want to sound stupid so he kept his mouth shut.

"What is your last name?" asked Rodrigo.

"Burnett."

"What kind of name is Burnett?"

Adam thought for a moment. No one had ever asked him that question.

"I don't know," he replied. "It's just a normal Canadian name, I think."

"Well, of course," said Rodrigo. "But there are no names that are *really* Canadian, right? Except for the Aboriginal people, I mean —"

Adam felt a little annoyed. How could Rodrigo think he already knew so much about Canada when he'd only arrived in the spring? "You know," he said, wanting to change the subject, "my family moved here a couple of weeks ago . . . from Castlegar."

"Is that a country?" Rodrigo looked confused.

"No, it's in Canada. It's a small town in the mountains near —"

"Listen up!" bellowed Old Baldy from the front of the classroom. "I want your presentation ready by next Friday. No more class time.

Adam groaned. "Man, first class with this guy and homework already."

"Why don't you come over to my house after school?" suggested Rodrigo. "I just got a new computer. We could start on the project."

"Okay," said Adam, as the bell rang. "Might as well get it done. See you then."

★★★

Adam met Rodrigo next to the bike racks after school. Rodrigo led the way across the field and down a long narrow street.

It felt good to talk to someone again. After English class, Adam had sat through French and Social Studies. Without Rodrigo, he'd gone back to feeling like an alien in this new school.

It turned out that Rodrigo lived near the school too. His house was far larger than Adam's, and had a beautiful, perfectly cut lawn. A flashy blue BMW convertible was parked out front.

"Is that your dad's?" asked Adam, wide-eyed.

"Yeah," Rodrigo answered casually.

When Rodrigo opened the front door, a short plump woman in an apron was standing there. She was holding a vacuum cleaner.

"*Buenos días, señors,*" she said.

"*Buenos días*, Maria," replied Rodrigo. He pointed at Adam. "*Se llama Adam.*"

"Hi," said Adam awkwardly.

"Hey, let's go up to my room," said Rodrigo. He kicked off his shoes and led the way up the stairs to their right. Large paintings in gold frames decorated the walls. The carpet was white and spotlessly clean.

"Was that your mom?" whispered Adam at the top of the stairs.

Rodrigo laughed. "My mom? Adam, that's Maria, our housekeeper and cook."

Adam didn't know what to say. He'd never met someone with a housekeeper. Or a cook.

The door to Rodrigo's room was at the end of a long hallway.

"Whoa!" exclaimed Adam as they entered the large room. Hundreds of soccer players stared back at him from the walls, from the ceiling, from every possible angle. They wore red shirts, purple shirts, green-and-white-striped shirts. Some players were black. Others were white. A few were dark-haired and had tan skin, like Rodrigo. Two were Asian.

Almost every square centimetre of Rodrigo's room was covered with old newspaper clippings. Some were in Spanish, a few in English, and still others in languages Adam had never seen. Many of them were yellowed and crinkled.

"My parents hate this," said Rodrigo, pointing at his walls. "They say my room looks like the inside of a garbage can. But they said I can keep it this way as long as I don't mess up the rest of the house."

"You *really* like soccer," said Adam, staring up at the ceiling. He thought of his own room. There was one big poster of Jarome Iginla and another of Sidney Crosby. And his Calgary Flames calendar, of course. But nothing like this.

They sat at Rodrigo's desk. Adam opened his

backpack and pulled out a pen and a notebook.

There was a shiny black laptop on the desk. Rodrigo opened it and pressed the power button. "I don't want to do this," he groaned. "I hate presentations."

"I know. They suck," said Adam. "And I bet Old Baldy's a hard marker."

The laptop played a tune as Rodrigo's desktop appeared.

Surprise, surprise, thought Adam. *Another soccer player. This guy is seriously obsessed!*

"Hey," Rodrigo exclaimed, tapping the table. He turned toward Adam. "I've got it — we could do our assignment on Diego Forlan!"

Adam shook his head. "Who?"

Rodrigo repeated the words slowly. "Di-e-go. For-lan." He pointed at the screen. "Him!"

"A soccer player?" said Adam.

"You've never heard of him?" Rodrigo burst out. "Manchester United? Atlético Madrid? Top scorer at the World Cup?"

Rodrigo seemed to be speaking English, but for Adam, it might as well have been Chinese.

Adam shook his head. "I've heard of the World Cup," he said hopefully. "But I don't really know much about soccer. Who's Atlético Madrid? Is he good?"

Rodrigo stared at Adam as if he was from Mars. "It's a team," he said. "Not a person."

The room was silent for a long moment.

"I play hockey," said Adam at last. He couldn't think of anything else to say.

"Hockey?" exclaimed Rodrigo. "You mean the one on ice?"

"Yeah," said Adam. *What other hockey would I be talking about?*

"How can you play a sport on something so slippery?" said Rodrigo, but didn't wait for him to answer. "Hey, I've got an idea — let's do both. I'll talk about Forlan and you choose your favourite ice man."

Adam was pretty sure that no one would care about some random soccer player. But dividing up the project would make it easier. "Sounds good."

"Okay," said Rodrigo. "Email me your part when it's done." He closed the laptop. "Now do you want to play some FIFA or something?"

"Okay, I guess," said Adam. Any video game was better than homework. "But I've never really played it before. I'm much better at NHL Hockey."

They plopped down on some cushions in front of the large TV. Rodrigo crawled forward and switched on the game.

Spanish menus appeared onscreen. Rodrigo pressed a few buttons. A green field appeared, filled with players dressed in blue or red.

"You're red," said Rodrigo.

Right away, Rodrigo launched a player into Adam's goalkeeper, sending him flying. The referee flashed a red card and the player marched furiously off the field.

"What happened?" asked Adam.

"Roughing up the goalkeeper's an easy way to get red-carded. That means sent off for the whole game," said Rodrigo.

"Man," exclaimed Adam, "what a pansy sport! In hockey that'd only be two minutes in the penalty box."

Rodrigo dumped Adam's goalkeeper again and they both laughed.

"That is pretty sweet," chuckled Adam. "Show me how to do it."

Rodrigo pointed to a button on his controller.

Adam's forward chopped down Rodrigo's goalkeeper with a big sliding tackle.

"Sweet," repeated Adam, as his player received a red card.

The game soon ended because there weren't enough players left on the field.

"Back in Uruguay," said Rodrigo. "That sometimes happens in real matches. Especially when there are big brawls."

Adam was surprised. He'd never really thought of soccer players as tough guys before.

For the next game, they made a deal not to slice down any more goalkeepers. For teams, Rodrigo selected Uruguay and Adam chose Brazil. He remembered hearing somewhere that Brazil was pretty good.

Adam was good at video games. He had spent many hours thrashing Jonah at NHL Hockey. But Rodrigo had clearly played FIFA a lot. He easily smashed in four goals against Adam's Brazil team.

It was only a video game, but Adam had to admit that it looked pretty cool. And, listening to Rodrigo speak, he was quickly able to learn the names of all the positions on a soccer field. "Goalkeeper" and "defender" were almost the same as in hockey. "Midfielder" was pretty obvious. Forwards were called "strikers." Adam liked the sound of that word — *striker.*

On the screen, shots zinged off the strikers' boots. The goalkeepers soared through the air. Defenders and midfielders crunched together and tumbled to the ground.

Adam managed to tackle Rodrigo's striker and thump the ball forward. His player reached the ball first.

Adam saw the Uruguayan goalkeeper.

Don't look at the goalie, he reminded himself. *Look at the back of the net.*

He angled his controller toward the empty far corner of the net and pressed a button. His Brazilian striker jumped into the air and smashed the ball into the goal with his head.

"What a goal!" shouted Rodrigo.

"Thanks!" Adam beamed. "Have you ever done that in a real game? I mean, scored with your head?"

"Only twice," replied Rodrigo.

"It doesn't hurt?" asked Adam, thinking of gym class and his nose.

"Well, yeah," said Rodrigo, nodding. "A bit. But it's worth it."

The game finished. Rodrigo switched off the TV and turned to Adam. "Do you want to go outside for a kick-around?"

"A what?" Adam said.

"Go ... to ... the ... park ... and ... kick ... around ... a ... soccer ... ball," droned Rodrigo, as if Adam couldn't understand English.

"Soccer?" said Adam. "With just two people? Sounds boring."

"Just for a little bit?"

"Well, I guess so. The school field's right by my house anyway."

"Okay, cool," said Rodrigo. He grabbed a blue-and-white soccer ball and a pair of black soccer boots from behind his bed. "Let's go!"

5 THE SECRET STICK

The school field was empty when they arrived. Rodrigo slipped on his boots, then jogged a few steps forward. On the way, he scooped the ball into the air with his right foot. When it came down, he caught it neatly on his left.

Show-off, thought Adam.

Rodrigo passed Adam the ball. It bounced away off Adam's shin.

"You need to cushion it more," explained Rodrigo, going to retrieve the ball. He demonstrated. "Just let your body go loose."

Yeah, yeah, thought Adam. *As if I really care.* But when the next pass came, he tried to loosen up. The ball slipped through his legs.

He tried again. This time, the ball stopped in front of him.

"Nice one!" exclaimed Rodrigo. "Hey, let's try some shooting."

"Sure, whatever," said Adam. He shrugged. But

when he turned, he saw the gaping face of the goal. Remembering all the times he'd scored in hockey, Adam felt a surge of electricity in his muscles.

But Adam went in goal first.

"Ready?" said Rodrigo. Adam nodded. The ball sailed into the net, right above his head. Rodrigo whooped and shot again. Adam tried to dive to his right, just like the goalkeepers in the video game. The ball slithered under his body, into the net.

Shot after shot zipped past him. *Jonah must be crazy!* thought Adam. *Who would ever want to be a goalie in any sport? This sucks!*

"Damn, I thought you'd be a good goalkeeper," said Rodrigo. "You're tall enough."

"Can I try shooting instead?" asked Adam. "I've never really played in goal. In hockey, I mean."

They switched places.

Adam ran and swung his right foot as hard as he could. But his toe caught in the ground behind the ball, which trickled to Rodrigo.

Next time, Adam swung harder. Another slow trickler. He tried again. A weak looping shot. And again. The ball soared wide of the net.

"Come on, Adam!" he groaned at himself.

"Try to hit it with your laces, not your toe," suggested Rodrigo, passing the ball back.

Adam stopped the ball and thought for a moment. "*Take ten percent off the power of every shot,*" his father had once told him, "*and you'll be fifty percent more accurate.*"

He looked at the net. *This thing's huge!* he realized.

He glanced at the wide-open bottom right-hand corner, then down at the ball. *Don't try to kill it,* he told himself. He swung firmly with his right foot, but with control. His laces smashed into the ball.

Pong! His shot hit the inside of the post and rebounded into the net.

Rodrigo looked at him, wide-eyed. "Where did *that* come from?"

"I don't know," shrugged Adam. "All I really did was aim."

The next shot roared off his foot and rocketed into the top-left corner.

Rodrigo stood there for a moment, stunned. "You know what?" he said. "With a shot like that, you would scare a lot of goalkeepers."

He fetched the ball and was about to throw it back to Adam when his eyes suddenly lit up. "Hey!" he exclaimed. "Why don't you come out for the soccer team? Tryouts are on Monday."

Rodrigo rolled the ball out. Adam shot again. It smacked into the crossbar and the goal frame shuddered.

"You can't be serious," said Adam.

"Why not?" said Rodrigo.

"I totally suck," replied Adam. "I've never really played — except in PE."

"Well, your touch on the ball isn't great," admitted Rodrigo. "And your passing needs work. But you are bigger and stronger than anyone else in our grade. And look at that shot — you've got good power and you definitely know how to aim. You've got the ability. I can teach you the rest."

"I dunno," said Adam. "My dad's signed me up for a team in the Vancouver Elite Hockey League. It starts at the end of next week. It's pretty intense."

"You could just give soccer a try. Plus it would be good fitness training for hockey, right?"

Adam's stomach rumbled. He glanced at his watch. It was nearly six.

"Look, I'd better get going," he said, picking up the ball and tossing it to Rodrigo. "Dinner."

"Okay, cool," said Rodrigo. "But what about tryouts?"

"I'll think about it," said Adam.

They walked together across the field toward the road and Adam's house.

"Adam!" boomed a loud voice. It was Adam's dad, dressed in a suit and standing next to his car in the driveway. He glanced down at the soccer ball in Rodrigo's hands as they approached.

"Hi there," he said to Rodrigo. "Who're you?"

"I'm Rodrigo. I'm in Adam's class."

"Rogerino . . . what kind of name is that?"

"Uruguayan."

"What?"

"I'm from Uruguay."

"Mm-hmm," said Adam's father, still looking confused. He turned back to Adam. "Well, we'd better head inside for dinner, Adam. Your mom's ordered curry or some damn thing tonight. Still, food is food, and you need to build up your strength for hockey season, eh?"

Adam followed his dad up the front steps.

"Nice to meet you, Roderogo," said Adam's father, looking back over his shoulder.

Dinner was already on the table. Adam's mother was spooning what looked like red stew from a takeout container into bowls of rice. Dalal's Curry House was written on the side of the container.

"Hey guys," she chirped at them. "Ready for some curry?"

Adam wasn't sure. He'd never eaten Indian food before. But he was starving.

He sat down and picked up his fork. He took a big bite, then closed his eyes. He thought it just might be the best thing he'd ever tasted.

Next to Adam, Jonah was already shovelling curry and rice into his mouth.

"Whoa!" exclaimed their father after taking a bite. He drained his glass of water. "Burgers next time, eh, guys?"

Adam's and Jonah's mouths were too full to answer.

"I'm sure the boys will have the rest of yours if you don't want it," said their mother, smiling.

Adam looked hopefully at his father's plate. His father raised an eyebrow and plunged his fork into a piece of chicken.

"Well — I suppose it's not *that* bad," he said, speaking with his mouth full. "I just prefer normal Canadian food. Like we ate in Castlegar. "

"You seem to be managing okay with the curry," said Adam's mother. "And it's good to try new things, right, guys?"

Adam's father rolled his eyes. He turned to Adam. "Anyway — what's with the soccer session today, bud?" He pointed to his head and tapped it three times. "You feeling okay?"

"It was nothing," said Adam, shrugging. "Rodrigo and I were working on a school project at his house and got bored. He just suggested it."

"How'd you meet Rodrigo?" asked his mother.

Adam took a sip of water. "First he helped me find my homeroom this morning," he explained, "then we partnered up in PE class —"

"What are you doing in PE?" interrupted Adam's father.

"We're starting with soccer," said Adam quickly.

His father groaned. "More soccer? Honestly, I don't know why the schools don't stick to normal sports. What are they going to teach you — pretending you're hurt and rolling around on the ground and grabbing your leg like they do in Europe and South America?"

Jonah giggled and dropped his fork on the floor.

"Unlike hockey players, soccer players aren't covered up in pads," said Adam's mother. "Anyway, Adam, I'm glad you've already made a friend. I know you were a bit worried about not knowing anyone at school."

"Mom . . ." groaned Adam. But he knew she was right. He just hoped that Rodrigo actually wanted to be his friend.

"Where is it that Rogerino's from again, Adam?" asked his father.

"It's called Uruguay, I think."

"Why do people from poor countries always play soccer?" said Adam's dad, pushing the rest of his food aside. "I guess they can't afford anything better."

"Honestly, Bruce," said Adam's mother. "That's a silly thing to say. It's not as simple as that."

"Is Uruguay very poor?" asked Adam. Rodrigo's home sure wasn't a poor person's house. Poor people didn't own sports cars.

"Adam," said his father, "I'm glad you made a friend already at Point Grey. And he seemed like a nice kid and all but —"

"But what?" interrupted Adam's mother, looking straight at her husband.

"But . . ." Adam's father went on, stammering a little, "but . . . never mind. I'm happy that you made a friend too, Adam. I know starting at a new school isn't easy."

Adam's mother gave her husband a nasty look

before picking up some plates and taking them to the kitchen.

"Speaking of friends," said Adam's father after a silence that seemed to go on forever, "hockey starts soon. I'm sure you'll meet some good guys there. Tryouts a week Friday." He looked at Adam. "You ready to show them what you've got?"

"You bet, Dad," Adam said, trying to sound confident. *How good is this Elite League?* he wondered. He thought of his teammates back in Castlegar. Without their awesome passes, would he really be able to score so many goals? Without Jason and Graham behind him, could he really be sure that someone always had his back?

"Hey Dad," Jonah chimed in, "when's my hockey start?"

"End of the month, Jonester," replied his father.

"I found some hockey stuff on the Internet yesterday," said Jonah.

"But you've got all your brother's old stuff," said their father, shaking his head. "And besides, to be honest, money's too tight right now to buy you new stuff. What do you need, anyway?"

"Um ... well," said Jonah, looking down, "it's goalie stuff. But it's really cheap, Dad. Honest!"

Adam's father sighed. "Jonah, we went through this last season. No son of mine is going to be stuck in goal. You've got lots of potential as a defenceman. End of story."

Jonah stood up and stormed out of the room. The

sound of his bedroom door slamming shut echoed throughout the house.

"What on earth was that all about?" said Adam's mother, popping her head back into the dining room.

Adam's father shook his head. "Just moody."

"The goalie thing again?" she asked, frowning at her husband. She turned to Adam. "Hey, it's your turn for the dishes."

Adam groaned. He was sure it wasn't his turn. He trudged off to the kitchen and began filling the sink with soapy water.

Over the sound of the water, he could hear his parents talking quietly. It was about Jonah. Adam knew his mother supported his father's decision to stop Jonah from playing in goal. She didn't like the idea of all those pucks speeding toward her younger son's head. And she was worried that he wouldn't get enough exercise.

Adam knew this wasn't true. Being a goalie was hard work. Graham was the only fat goalie Adam had ever seen. And he was sort of a fit fat guy, really.

"Doing okay, bud?" said Adam's father, strolling into the kitchen.

"Yeah," Adam, rinsing off a plate.

Adam's father leaned against the kitchen counter. "So," he said, his voice hushed, "I stopped by a sports store after work today. They just got a whole shipment of composite sticks. You know — the new, shiny, gold super-light ones?"

"Really?" said Adam. Sidney Crosby and Jarome Iginla used those sticks.

"Well, bud, I know moving away from your friends has been tough. And I know you're probably a little nervous about the Elite League," said his father. He reached into his pocket and took out his wallet. He held ten $20 bills toward Adam. "I think one of those sticks would really give you an edge."

Adam hesitated for a moment. "I thought you said money was tight," he said. "I don't want to cause you or Mom any problems."

"It's okay — we'll make do," his father replied. "But just for now, maybe we should keep this between the two of us, okay?"

Uncertainly, Adam took the money and slipped it into his pocket. *It's only paper*, he told himself. But somehow the wad of bills felt heavy, as if it was dragging him down.

6 SORTA LIKE A SOCCER PLAYER

On Monday after school, Adam sat alone in the school changing room, head in his hands.

At least he'd had PE that day — PE and English were the only classes he shared with Rodrigo. On Friday, he hadn't talked to anyone all day.

And the weekend, he thought. *Man oh man, was that brutal.* He'd felt so bored and lonely that he'd actually hung out with Jonah. He'd wanted to call Rodrigo, but he didn't have his number. And he didn't want to seem lame or desperate.

Adam stood up and glanced at his reflection in the mirror. In his black gym shorts and red Calgary Flames t-shirt, he didn't look much like a soccer player.

What am I thinking? he wondered for the hundredth time that day.

Outside, light rain sprinkled down on the field. All around Adam, other players were already jogging around and stretching. Near the far goal, a group of about six stood in a circle, making sharp little passes.

Adam spotted Rodrigo putting on his boots. He walked over to his friend. "I can't believe you talked me into this," he said.

Rodrigo grinned. He handed Adam a pair of blue soccer socks and two very small pieces of plastic.

"What are these for?" asked Adam.

"Coach won't let you play without shin pads," said Rodrigo. "Sorry, these are my old ones."

Adam turned one of the flimsy pads over in his hand. "Good thing soccer's such a girly sport," he scoffed. "You'd get killed if you played hockey in these."

"Why do hockey players wear all that equipment?" teased Rodrigo. "Can't they take a tackle?"

"Tackle? You mean a bodycheck," said Adam. He strapped the small shin pads onto his legs, then pulled the socks over them.

"Nice!" laughed Rodrigo. "You look sorta like a soccer player!" He pulled a pair of black soccer boots out of his bag, then slapped his thigh. "Adam — I didn't realize you had feet like water skis! These will never fit!"

"So?" said Adam, pointing to his running shoes. "I'll just wear these."

"You need soccer boots to play soccer," said Rodrigo. "Would you play ice hockey without skates?"

A whistle blew behind them. Adam turned in surprise. It was Mr. McKay, standing next to a bag of soccer balls and a stack of orange cones. "Everybody in!" he boomed. "Hustle!"

The players gathered around the coach. Rodrigo dropped to one knee. Adam did the same.

Coach McKay did a quick head count. "Twenty-five!" he called out. "Well, fellas, welcome to tryouts for the Point Grey Dragons. You'd better show me what you can do. We can only take sixteen players."

"Tyler! Jit!" he barked, gesturing to a slim blond boy and a short, muscular South Asian kid. "Take these guys for a run!"

Adam looked down. His hands were shaking a little. His stomach felt like it was spinning and wouldn't stop.

"Let's go!" said Rodrigo, slapping him on the shoulder.

"Two lines behind us!" called Tyler from the front.

Adam gritted his teeth and ran harder, catching up to the player in front of him.

"What part of the word 'line' don't you understand?" Tyler shouted.

Adam got back in line. He glared at the back of Tyler's blond head. *Better watch your mouth, kid,* he thought.

After jogging four laps, they stopped to stretch. And stretch. And stretch. Adam didn't think he'd ever stretched so much in his life.

"All right, last one," called Jit, clapping his hands. "Everyone on the line."

"Argh," groaned Rodrigo quietly. "Sprints."

They split into six groups of five. Coach McKay set

out four cones in front of each group.

"Last group does double pushups," he said. "Go!"

Off they went. First cone, back. Second cone, back. *No problem,* thought Adam. *Just like skating the lines at hockey.*

Rodrigo finished, and Adam exploded forward. He reached the first cone well ahead of everyone else. He planted his left leg to turn.

Whoosh! Adam was suddenly on his back, staring up at the grey sky. Behind him, raucous laughter filled the air. He felt his face burn red, but rolled over quickly and leaped to his feet. He sprinted after the other players, straining every muscle to catch up.

But he just couldn't turn. Twice more, he slipped in the wet grass and fell. And twice more, everyone laughed at him. He finished last.

"All right, twenty pushups, everyone," said Coach McKay. "Except Jit's group. You've got forty."

All around Adam, his group groaned.

One, two — they began the pushups. Adam closed his eyes, breathing out every time he pushed away from the ground.

Nine, ten . . .

Adam saw Rodrigo's arms start to shake. *Already?* he thought. *This is easy!*

Twenty-one . . . twenty-two . . .

The other groups were finished.

Thirrr . . . ty-nine . . . forrr . . . ty!

Everyone in Adam's group collapsed onto the ground around him.

"How were the pushups, Jit-o?" chuckled a voice from above. Adam looked up. It was Tyler.

"Hey—give me a break," replied Jit. "Look at my team!" He pointed at Adam mockingly. "He can't even stand up." He nodded in Rodrigo's direction. "And that kid did half of his pushups granny-style."

Adam clenched his fists.

"Time for a game!" shouted Coach McKay. He started splitting them into four teams.

"All right, last team —" said Coach McKay, "— Adam, Rodrigo, Alex, Mason, Nima, Kai, and . . . Jit!"

Jit held up his hands in dismay. Tyler laughed at him.

Two games kicked off, side by side. Adam's team wore blue bibs against Tyler's team, who wore red.

"You're up front," said Rodrigo to Adam quietly. "I'll pass it to you. Just try to get open."

Same as hockey, thought Adam. *Get open, shoot, score.*

To start, Rodrigo passed the ball back to Jit, who dribbled around one of the Red Bibs easily. Adam jogged toward the Red Bibs' goal. Jit pushed the ball back to his goalkeeper, who kicked it long toward Adam.

Adam stuck out his right leg to cushion the ball, just like Rodrigo had taught him. But a boot slipped in front of his and knocked the ball away. At the same time, a shoulder crunched against him, sending him sprawling on the ground.

"Nice, Tyler!" shouted Coach McKay. "Great timing!"

The ball flew toward Adam's chest. Tyler ducked in front of him and headed the ball away. It landed at the feet of a short, speedy Reds player. The speedster zipped past two Blues defenders, then smashed the ball into the roof of the net.

Another pass from Rodrigo slipped through Adam's legs. Tyler passed it forward. The speedy striker for the Blues scored again, this time with a clever flick.

Adam swore under his breath.

The ball switched from Reds to Blues and back again. Adam ran around as fast as he could. He couldn't seem to stop slipping and falling. And he couldn't seem to get the ball.

A long clearance landed on Tyler's right knee. He got the ball to drop perfectly in front of him. Rodrigo slid in with a crunching tackle that sent the blond boy tumbling. He nipped the ball between a Reds defender's legs and spun past another. He passed to Adam.

"Adam," called Jit, "over here!"

No, this is my chance! thought Adam. He swung his leg as hard as he could.

The ball sliced off his foot, sailing wildly over the net. It bounced off one of the trees that lined the far end of the park.

Adam looked sideways. Jit was standing six metres from the goal, completely open.

"C'mon, man — have a look!" Jit shouted, holding up his hands.

Tweeee! Coach McKay's whistle sounded. "Okay, guys, good effort today," he said. "One more tryout session. Next Monday's your last chance to impress."

"Last chance," whispered Jit quietly as he walked past Adam. "Better find yourself a pair of boots."

★★★

A few days later, the Number 7 bus pulled up to the stop where Adam and Rodrigo were waiting. They climbed on board, and Rodrigo dumped a handful of coins into the box next to the driver. It beeped and gave him a ticket.

Adam handed the driver a $5 bill from his wallet.

"What am I supposed to do with this?" asked the driver. He pointed at the *Exact Change Only* sign.

Rodrigo inserted change into the box until it beeped again. He handed the ticket to Adam.

"Here's your five bucks back, son," said the driver. "Unless you're trying to tip me."

The bus moved forward.

"Thanks," said Adam as they found seats. He tried to give the $5 bill to Rodrigo.

"No, don't worry about it, man," said Rodrigo. "You can buy me a Gatorade later. Never been on a bus?"

"Not in Vancouver," Adam said. He didn't want Rodrigo to know that he'd never been on a public bus before. The public bus in Castlegar only ran five or six times a day. Adam didn't know anyone who actually used it.

Adam watched the buildings get bigger and bigger as the bus got closer to downtown.

"Do you know when to get off?" he asked Rodrigo.

"Three more stops," said his friend.

A few minutes later, Rodrigo pressed a button and the bus stopped.

PACIFIC CENTRE MALL, said a huge sign on the building in front of them.

Rodrigo led the way through a set of large glass doors. Adam couldn't believe how busy it was. Everywhere he looked, there were stores. Stores and teenagers.

"How'd you figure out this city so fast?" Adam asked Rodrigo as they walked. "I mean, buses and stuff. You only got here in May, right?"

"I've lived in Uruguay, France, Brazil, and the United States. So I'm used to finding my way around in new places."

Adam nodded. He suddenly envied his friend. Rodrigo was the same age as he was, but he'd been to so many more places and seen so many different things. At the same time, Adam felt a bit sorry for Rodrigo. He remembered how hard it had been to leave his friends in Castlegar. What would it be like to do that over and over again?

"To tell you the truth," added Rodrigo, "I didn't have much to do this summer. My parents both go away on business a lot. And I didn't really know anyone yet. So I just explored."

A group of cute girls walked past. Rodrigo and Adam turned to look. Adam gave Rodrigo a secretive thumbs-up and they both laughed.

"Hey, look," said Rodrigo suddenly, nudging him and pointing.

Adam looked. Walking toward them were Tyler and Jit.

"Hey," said Rodrigo casually.

"What's up, guys?" said Jit. Tyler only nodded as they walked by.

"Rodrigo, those guys are jerks," said Adam. "That Tyler guy thinks he's all that."

"I'm not so sure," said Rodrigo. "The season was over last year when I came. So just like you, I'm new. Tyler and Jit are grade tens, so this is their third year playing for the Dragons. It's their team. Would you be friendly to a new guy trying out for your hockey team?"

"Especially a new guy who sucks," said Adam, nodding.

"You didn't *completely* suck," joked Rodrigo.

"Yeah right," replied Adam bitterly. "I guess I'm just not a soccer player."

"Look, Jit made fun of me too," replied Rodrigo, "because I couldn't do pushups. I may have skill, but I wish I had your speed and strength. Every team needs a big guy up front."

Rodrigo stopped at a store called AllSports.

"But," he said firmly, "you'll need a proper pair of boots."

Adam shook his head. "Forget it. I haven't got the money, anyway."

"Ask your parents?" Rodrigo suggested.

Adam imagined his father's reaction if he asked for money to buy soccer boots. *Not an option*, he thought. "See, hockey starts tomorrow. So there's no point in —"

Suddenly, he remembered the stick money.

"What?" said Rodrigo, seeing Adam's expression change.

Adam took out his wallet. He showed Rodrigo the $200 his father had given him.

"See? No problem," said Rodrigo. "You can get a decent pair of boots for sixty bucks."

"My dad gave it to me for a new hockey stick," Adam explained. He pointed to a row of gleaming gold-coloured sticks in the store window. "Like those." Then he added, "And my dad hates soccer."

"I've got it!" burst out Rodrigo, walking into the store. "Let's go have a look."

"But my dad —" began Adam, following reluctantly.

"Look," said Rodrigo, turning to Adam. "My dad

makes me work for my allowance. You know, to teach me the value of money." He rolled his eyes. "So anyway, Last night he phoned from New York. He said he has a special job for me. And he said if I could get a friend to help, he would pay us eighty dollars. Each!"

"Really?" exclaimed Adam. "When?"

"He doesn't get back from his business trip until the weekend after this one," said Rodrigo, shaking his head. "So you'd only have to keep it a secret for a little over a week."

"Hmm," said Adam. "I guess I could just say that the sticks at the store didn't have the right curve. I'll tell him I had to order a special one." He felt a pang of guilt. He didn't want to lie to his father, but couldn't think of any other way.

"Well then, problem solved," said Rodrigo.

At the back wall of the store, there was a huge display of soccer boots of all types and colours. Rodrigo began grabbing boots off the shelf. He held each one up to his eye, like a scientist examining a test tube.

Adam snatched a shiny purple boot from its perch. "Who would ever wear this?" he demanded, raising both eyebrows. "It looks like a ballet slipper."

"Messi wore those boots in the World Cup," said Rodrigo.

"His name is Messy?" asked Adam.

"Lionel Messi — he's the best player in the world!" exclaimed Rodrigo, shaking his head.

"Whatever," said Adam, putting the boot back. "I'm not wearing those."

"Good," replied Rodrigo. "They cost three hundred dollars. How about these?" He handed a pair of black-and-white Adidas boots to Adam, and pointed at the six long metal spikes on them.

"Sweet!" exclaimed Adam, taking the boots in his hands. "These cleats are huge!"

"Cleats?" said Rodrigo, looking confused. "Oh, you mean studs. Yeah, these will really dig in. Better not slide into anyone with your studs up, though. You'll be red-carded straightaway."

Adam sat down to try them on.

He laced up one boot, then the other, then stood up. He bounced a few times and walked around a little.

"So, what do you think?" asked Rodrigo.

"Yeah," said Adam, unable to hide his smile. "These are the ones."

7 THE ELITE LEAGUE

"Dude, I dunno about a kick-around tonight," said Adam the next day after school. "I've got hockey tonight at seven-thirty."

"Just for a bit?" pleaded Rodrigo. "We'll take it easy, I promise. You've got to break in the new boots before the next tryout."

"Okay, okay," sighed Adam, pulling the boots out of his locker. He was keeping them at school. He couldn't risk his father finding them at home.

There was a girls' soccer practice on the school field.

"It's okay," said Rodrigo. "I know a little soccer pitch near here."

"Pitch?" asked Adam, confused. His mind was filled with thoughts of baseball.

"Ah, sorry," said Rodrigo. "In soccer, we call a field a pitch."

They walked to an elementary school near Rodrigo's house. Adam smiled when he saw that there was, in fact, a baseball field right in the middle of the soccer pitch.

"Well, that sucks," said Rodrigo, scuffing the baseball pitcher's mound with his left foot. "Imagine tripping over that!"

"You could take a good shot off there," joked Adam. "It'd be just like a golf tee."

Rodrigo tried. The ball soared into the top corner of the goal. "You might be right," he said with a grin.

Adam loved the way his studded boots bit into the grass, just like newly sharpened skates carving through ice. He could cut right, cut left, pivot, and stop on a dime.

Rodrigo passed him the ball. It bounced off the side of his toe.

"Let's just shoot," he said to Rodrigo.

"How about you pass me the ball and I pass it back. You control it, then shoot," said Rodrigo, walking to the front of the goal. "That's more realistic. More like a game."

Rodrigo's first two passes sailed past Adam.

"What are you doing?" called Adam. "Your passes are all over the place!"

"Trying to get you to move," said Rodrigo.

Adam understood right away. What did his father always say? *The puck won't find you if you stand around waiting for it.*

He moved quickly to receive the next pass. It flicked up into the air off his left boot. *Ninety percent*, he thought. He smashed it out of mid-air.

"Hey!" hollered Rodrigo. He was holding his hand between his knees. The ball was in the back of the net.

"Sorry, man," said Adam, cringing.

"No, no — great shot!" said Rodrigo, wringing his hand. "I'm no goalkeeper, that's all. What did you do differently that time?"

"I don't know," said Adam. "I think I just relaxed. And moved to get into position."

He smashed another scorcher into the goal. Rodrigo dived out of the way.

"Try a header," he hollered, tossing the ball toward Adam's head.

"No way!" shouted Adam, ducking. "Can't I be a soccer player without the heading?"

"Look at how tall you are!" said Rodrigo. "You'll be an absolute beast up front if you can head the ball. It's not that bad. The power comes from your legs." He demonstrated, bending his knees and flexing his back, then snapping his body forward. "And whatever you do, force yourself to keep your eyes open."

He tossed the ball toward Adam again.

Do it! Adam told himself. *Eyes open!*

He jumped toward the ball. It crashed into his forehead and flew into the net.

"See?" said Rodrigo. "It's as easy as that."

"Yeah — not so bad," said Adam, rubbing his head. It hadn't exactly felt good. Suddenly he glanced down at his watch.

"Oh no!" he exclaimed. "It's almost six! Have we really been out here two hours?"

Adam sprinted over to where he'd left his backpack. He tugged off his boots and crammed them inside. *So much for keeping them at school tonight*, he thought. *And so much for getting home before Dad*. Adam wasn't looking forward to another conversation with his father about playing soccer with Rodrigo.

"I think you can make the soccer team, Adam," said Rodrigo as they walked quickly toward their neighbourhood. "Really. You've got a chance."

"Aw, c'mon," replied Adam. *My ball control's awful,* he told himself. But he wondered if Rodrigo might be right. His shooting had improved. And his passing was slowly getting better.

"You know," said Rodrigo, "everyone thinks soccer is all about clever little flicks and tricks. That stuff's useful — but I think being tough is more important. And playing your part in the team."

Easy for him to say, thought Adam. *He's got all the flicks and tricks*. But what Rodrigo said stuck in his mind.

They reached Rodrigo's house. "Good luck at hockey," said Rodrigo, waving. "Don't slip on the ice."

Adam rushed off.

When he got home, the door was unlocked. His father was sitting in the living room with Jonah, watching Canadian football on TV.

"Where've you been?" he demanded. He pointed

at Adam's legs, which were caked with dirt and grass.

"Oh — I did some jogging and, um . . . sprints on a field by Rodrigo's house," said Adam, wishing that he didn't have to lie. "Just getting ready for the hockey season."

He shifted his backpack uncomfortably and the studs of his boots scraped against his back. Wincing slightly, Adam wondered if his father had already guessed that he'd been playing soccer again.

But his father just shook his head. "Adam," he groaned, "is that really the best idea right before hockey tryouts? Hurry up. You've barely got time to eat before we go."

As he left the room, Adam breathed a huge sigh of relief.

★★★

Twenty minutes later, they were on their way to the Kerrisdale Arena.

"Feelin' good, bud?" asked Adam's father. He was gripping the steering wheel very tightly, Adam noticed. His knuckles were white.

"Yeah, Dad, of course," he said. "I can't wait!"

"Pasta was okay?" his father asked.

"Yeah, fine, Dad," he answered.

His father looked almost, well, nervous. *What's with him?* Adam wondered. *It's not like he's going to be playing.*

"Hey," said his father as they turned into the arena parking lot. He spoke quietly so that Jonah, in the back seat, couldn't hear. "You get the stick?"

"None had quite the right curve," said Adam, feeling a guilty lump in his throat. "I ordered one in."

"Good call," his father said. "Important to get it just right."

Adam got out of the car, relieved again that his father hadn't caught on to his lies. He picked up his bag and his old stick. "I've scored plenty of goals with this one too, right?"

"That's my boy!" said his father.

When Adam pushed open the doors of the Kerrisdale Arena, the unmistakable stale odour of hockey equipment filled his nose. The air was crisp and cold. The reality hit him and his heart beat fast.

Hockey starts tonight!

"Adam," said his father, looking straight at him. "Do your best." He turned to Jonah. "Hey, let's go get a hot chocolate, little buddy."

Adam saw a sign with an arrow marked ELITE LEAGUE TRYOUTS — CHANGING ROOM 6.

He thought of the changing rooms back in Castlegar. Jason — strutting by, whacking everyone's shin pads and shouting encouragement. Graham the goalie — asking someone to help do up his leg pads. He could almost hear the blare of heavy-metal music. He remembered what it had felt like to celebrate that final win with his friends.

Kerrisdale Arena's Changing Room 6 was almost silent when he entered. The only sounds were of pads being strapped on and tape wrapping around legs. There were green and red practice jerseys hung up around the room. Adam took a seat under red shirt Number 9 and started getting dressed.

A huge, dark-haired guy entered the dressing room. "*I'm* Number 9," he said, stepping in front of Adam.

Adam was about to argue but decided against it. He didn't want to cause trouble on his first day. "Sure, man, whatever," he managed to say. He moved sideways and sat under red Number 10.

He looked around the big changing room. Everyone was huge, even the goalies, and not in a Graham-the-fat-goalie kind of way.

Adam began lacing up his skates.

One by one, silently, players started to leave the room. Adam followed.

When his skates hit the ice, his muscles suddenly felt charged, electric. He surged forward, large bodies swerving and cutting around him. He slowed slightly and looked up. There were at least forty players on the ice.

Twee!

"Everyone in!"

The players all gathered around the large man standing at centre ice. He had a red, bulbous nose and a thick moustache, and was wearing a track suit and baseball hat.

"I'm Coach Wilson!" he barked. "Half of you will make this team. Eighteen skaters, two goalies. If you make the cut, you will be playing some of the best teams in the province, maybe even the country. I don't care who you are. I don't care how many goals you scored on some wimpy house league team last year. *You* need to show me that *you* are better than everyone else. You're not little boys anymore. You're men. I've got no time to be nice."

After the warm-up, Coach Wilson and his assistant lined them up for some one-on-one skating.

"Make no mistake," said the head coach. "This is a race."

Adam found himself at the front of the line. He was up against a short, stocky kid in a white helmet.

Twee! They surged ahead. Adam's blades carved into the ice. He cut around the first circle, and ripped around the second.

First blue line. Second blue line.

Go, go, go!

As he streaked toward the far goal line, Adam saw his opponent edging ahead. He pumped his legs harder, but it wasn't enough. The guy in the white helmet zipped across the line first.

Races continued. Coach Wilson and his assistant stood in the Home bench, watching carefully and making notes on clipboards.

Adam won his next five races, although not by

much. He couldn't get the guy in the white helmet out of his mind. In Castlegar, nobody had ever been able to catch Adam.

"All right!" barked the coach. "Time for a game."

The Reds and Greens skated to separate benches.

"Here's the lineup," said Coach Wilson's assistant, reading from his clipboard. Reds clustered around. Adam saw his name.

First line, centre.

"What the hell!" grumbled someone next to him. It was the guy in the white helmet. "I'm second line?" He poked Adam in the chest. "But I beat you in that race."

"I didn't choose the lineup," said Adam.

The player glared back at him, looking like he was ready to drop his gloves and fight.

A whistle sounded behind them, and Adam skated away.

Coach Wilson dropped the puck at centre ice. Adam won the opening faceoff and sent the puck over to his big, beefy right winger.

Adam elbowed past the Green centre and headed straight for their defensive zone.

"Over here," he shouted. "I'm open!"

The boy looked right at him. But instead of passing, he tried to deke past a big Green defenceman. The defenceman shouldered him to the ice and passed the puck forward.

Racing back to help out, Adam caught up to

the Green puck-carrier. He smashed the player into the boards. Glancing up, he scooped the puck forward to his speedy left winger, then raced after his teammate.

"Hey!" hollered Adam, as they crossed the blue line. "Over here, man!"

Like the first player, the left winger looked at Adam but didn't pass. Instead he managed to slip past a defenceman and squeeze off a weak shot. The Green goalie caught it easily.

Adam slammed his stick on the ice. *Why won't anyone pass?*

His line skated to the bench for a change.

"Hey guys," said Adam to his linemates as they sat down, "we can beat them if we pass more."

"Shut up, man," said the big, beefy right winger. "I wanna show the coach what I can do. I don't care about you."

"Yeah," sneered the left winger. "I'm not here to make you look good. I've got scouts from junior teams looking at me already, you know."

And I thought this was a team sport, thought Adam bitterly. He gripped his stick more tightly.

"First line!" hollered the assistant coach. Adam leaped over the boards. He thumped into a large Green and knocked him sprawling. Flying through the neutral zone, he spotted the mouthy right winger next to him.

He hesitated for a moment, then passed the puck.

"Over here!" shouted Adam, surging toward the Green net.

The winger ignored him and took a slapshot. It thumped off the goalie's pads right to Adam. Snapping his wrists quickly, he roofed it over the goalie's glove hand.

He pumped his fist in the air and turned around. Where were his teammates? No one had come to congratulate him. In fact, they were already skating away!

There wasn't one single high-five when he got to the bench.

The game ended 1–0. Adam left the ice with the rest of the players.

In the changing room once again, only ripping tape and the crackle of Velcro straps broke the silence.

Coach Wilson entered the room. "Gentlemen," he announced, "it is time for the first cut. We will call ten players into the other room, one by one. If you are called, you are not one of the thirty who will progress to the second tryout."

He left, and it went even quieter in the changing room.

"Jeez, this is intense," whispered Adam to the boy next to him.

"Shut up, man. No one cares what you think," snapped the boy, turning away.

"Yeah," chimed in the big, beefy right-winger from Adam's team, "puck hog."

Puck hog? thought Adam. *I was the only one who passed at all!*

One player was called out. When he returned to the changing room, it was only to pick up his bag and storm out, swearing loudly.

Eight more names were called and eight more players left, cursing and slamming doors.

A last player was called. When he came back, he was crying.

"Want a tissue, Baby Face?" someone laughed. Chuckles erupted around the changing room.

What kind of team is this? thought Adam.

8 USING YOUR HEAD

"Hey, you ready for today?" called Rodrigo.

Adam was too busy wrestling with his huge school bag to answer. It was full of books and soccer equipment and wouldn't quite fit into his locker. He pushed the door hard, then quickly fastened the lock with his free hand.

"Nice," said Rodrigo, nodding approvingly.

"Ready, yeah," replied Adam. "You got my email, right?" He had actually spent some time over the weekend on their presentation and didn't want it to go to waste.

"Yeah, yeah, yeah." Rodrigo held up a small, blue USB stick shaped like a soccer ball. "But who cares about that? What about soccer tryouts? You ready?"

Adam pointed to his locker. "I've got boots this time, at least," he said as they headed for English class.

In the classroom, Old Baldy had written a list of names on the board. Adam and Rodrigo's presentation was second to last.

"I was hoping to get it over with early," complained Adam.

A small, freckly girl and her tall, bony friend were first. They gave a very long presentation about the freckly girl's cat. Although he wasn't technically a person, they said, they both admired him greatly for many different reasons, which they began to explain in great detail.

Halfway through the girls' second slide, Adam put one elbow on his desk. He leaned his cheek against his hand and closed his eyes. This was going to be a *long* lesson.

"Wake up, Adam!" snapped Old Baldy. "That's very rude."

Adam made a face at Rodrigo. Rodrigo made a dozy face back.

The presentations went on and on. One was on Nickelback, a band Adam hated. Another was on J.K. Rowling, presented by two boys who seemed to know absolutely everything about Harry Potter.

"Adam, Rodrigo — you're next," said their teacher.

A classroom full of bored faces stared back at Adam when he got to the front. Adam realized he could barely remember what he'd planned to say.

Rodrigo loaded the presentation onto the laptop at the front of the room. He clicked, and the name DIEGO FORLAN appeared at the top of the screen.

"I'd like to tell you all about my favourite soccer player," Rodrigo began. "But I think it's better if I let his boots speak for him."

He clicked again and a video appeared.

Onscreen, the same soccer player from Rodrigo's desktop stood behind a soccer ball. His long blond hair was held back with a headband.

Oh man, thought Adam, looking around the room. *Look at this guy! We're gonna get laughed off the face of the earth.*

Suddenly there was a burst of loud electronic music. The whole class jerked upright in their seats.

Onscreen, the small blond man jogged forward and thumped the ball with his right foot. It swerved over a wall of defenders and bent into the top corner of the net. The man sprinted away cheering madly. His teammates chased after him, tugging at his blue jersey and slapping him on the back.

"Cool!" exclaimed a guy at the back of the class.

The video sped up, flashing through three more incredible goals.

The music stopped. The word GOAL appeared in huge white letters in front of a blue background.

"What did you guys think of those goals?" asked Rodrigo.

"Awesome!" said someone.

"Wicked!"

"Well," said Rodrigo, grinning broadly, "I completely agree. But those goals are not the only reason I chose Forlan as the person I admire most."

He pressed a button.

Forlan appeared again, sprinting toward a huge goal-keeper. This time, he faked the shot and slid the ball sideways. His teammate tapped the ball into an empty net.

The video switched to Forlan sliding in for a tough tackle. Blood oozing from a cut on his knee, he jumped up and chipped the ball over a defender. A big, lanky teammate smashed it into the net.

The player ran to Forlan and they embraced.

Rodrigo clicked one more time and the last slide appeared. It was a map of South America. Uruguay was labelled, and highlighted in blue.

"Everyone in the world has heard of Canada," said Rodrigo, "and America, Australia, France. But when I tell people I am Uruguayan, they look at me like I'm from another planet. Even if they've heard of my country, they know nothing about it. Most people know that Canada has maple syrup and hockey and Bryan Adams — and that you have French-speaking people here as well as English. But nobody knows anything about Uruguay.

"Diego Forlan scores great goals, sure. But he also passes, he tackles, and he runs for miles and miles. He fights for his teammates and for his country. When I see him play, it reminds me that there are many good things in Uruguay, not only problems. He makes me proud to be Uruguayan."

All around the class, students murmured excitedly.

"Shhh!" went Old Baldy.

"And now Adam's going to talk about his favourite hockey player," Rodrigo announced. He clicked a button on the laptop. A somewhat fuzzy picture of Sidney Crosby taking a slapshot appeared on the screen.

"So, um, yeah . . ." began Adam. "This is Sidney Crosby."

The room had fallen silent again. In the back, someone coughed.

"Sidney Crosby was born in . . ." said Adam slowly, reading from his notes.

This isn't going to work, he thought.

Suddenly he knew what he had to do.

"Look," he said, "to be honest, my presentation isn't worth listening to. All I was planning to talk about was Sidney Crosby's Olympic gold medal–winning goal and his very impressive stats.

"But when I heard Rodrigo's presentation just now," Adam explained, "I realized that I don't just admire Sidney Crosby for one goal — or even for all his goals."

He paused for a moment and looked around. His classmates weren't exactly ready to break into a standing ovation, but they were listening.

"In some ways," said Adam, taking a deep breath, "Crosby is a lot like Forlan. Crosby fights for the puck in the corners. He sticks up for his teammates when the other team gets rough. And he knows when to shoot and when to pass the puck.

"I always used to believe," he continued, "that hockey was better than soccer because it was our sport and it was Canadian. But learning about Forlan today — I'm starting to think that maybe the important thing is not so much which sport you play — or even which country you come from . . ." Adam looked over at Old Baldy nervously.

His English teacher had stopped writing notes. Now he was doing something that Adam had never seen him do. He was smiling.

". . . Maybe it's the people you play with."

★★★

"Come on, guys!" shouted Coach McKay. "Push it!"

Adam dug deep and pushed ahead, leading his team through the final sprint. It was raining again and the ground was slippery. But this time as he ran, Adam could feel the studs on his boots biting into the ground — and it felt great.

"Quality, Adam — nice effort," said a voice next to him when he reached the goal line. A hand patted him on the back.

Adam looked up. It was Jit.

"Th-thanks, man," he replied, feeling warm despite the rain.

I've got to make this team, he told himself. He didn't care anymore that it was a soccer team and not a hockey team. He just wanted to play on a team with these guys. He wanted them to be his friends.

The players gathered inside a large rectangle of small green cones.

"Pass, then move," explained Coach McKay. He knocked a ball toward Tyler and sprinted away. "Tyler!" he called.

The blond boy sent over a pass, but it was way out of Coach McKay's reach.

"Rodrigo—you try!" shouted Coach McKay. Adam's friend sent a perfect pass that sizzled along the turf. It landed right on the coach's left foot.

"That," said Coach McKay, pointing, "is how to make a pass."

He turned toward Tyler. "Hey!" he called. "What are you waiting for? Go get the ball! And two laps — that pass was horrible."

Tyler jogged away, muttering under his breath.

The drill started. "C'mon guys," shouted Coach McKay. "No one's going to give you the ball for free in this game. Move, move, move!"

Adam sprinted back and forth. He found a team-mate. The pass thudded off his shin pad. The next pass hit his knee and flew away. Another pass nearly tripped him.

After a few minutes, the coach's whistle blew. Adam swore under his breath. He hadn't controlled the ball once.

"Headers, guys," said Coach McKay. "Adam, come here a sec," he added, beckoning.

Adam jogged over.

"Listen," said the coach. "You've got to improve your touch. The ball keeps bouncing off you. You're fast and strong and you work hard. But if you're all tensed up, the ball won't stick.

"I heard you play hockey," the coach went on. "Well, cushioning the puck with your stick's the same thing as your touch on the ball. When the pass comes to you, relax. It'll stick to you like Velcro."

Adam nodded. The coach blew his whistle loudly.

"Time for a game!" he bellowed.

The teams were the same as the week before. Rodrigo, Adam, and the Blue Bibs found themselves facing off against Tyler and his Red Bibs.

Rodrigo looked at Adam and clenched his fists. "Let's show them what we can do. Head for the penalty area and I'll find you."

Adam looked at him blankly. "Where?"

"The penalty area — the big box around the goal," explained Rodrigo.

The short speedy striker on the Reds kicked off to Tyler. Adam sprinted forward, closing him down.

"Man on, Tyler!" shouted one of the Red Bibs. Tyler spun around. Adam clattered into his thigh, sending him flying.

"Free kick to the Red Bibs!" hollered Coach McKay.

"That's all right," said Rodrigo quietly to Adam. "You have to let them know we mean business. Come on, it's a free kick for them. Help me make a wall in case they shoot."

He pulled Adam next to him with two other players. "Cover your balls," he whispered, "just in case."

Adam thought Rodrigo was joking and laughed out loud.

"Seriously," said Rodrigo, holding his hands in front of his crotch.

Adam hurried to do the same.

Tyler hammered the ball with his right foot. It soared toward Adam's head. Every instinct told Adam to duck. But he remembered Rodrigo's words from the presentation earlier that day.

Gotta take one for the team, he thought.

He stood fast. The ball glanced off his forehead. He tumbled backwards.

"You all right, Adam?" asked Rodrigo, offering him a hand up.

"I think so," said Adam. "Didn't hurt as much as I thought it would." He rubbed his forehead. It had hurt quite a bit.

"Get up there, Blues!"

Adam looked behind him. He saw Nobu, their goalkeeper, with the ball. After it had hit Adam's head, the ball had flown right into the keeper's hands.

Nobu punted the ball. It looped in a high arc and found Rodrigo alone on the left side. The ball hit his chest and dropped to the ground in front of him.

Adam rushed up the field at top speed.

"Adam!" shouted Rodrigo. "Go! Penalty area!" He pushed the ball past a Red Bibs defender and knocked it across the pitch.

The ball skipped off the wet grass. It reached Adam just below knee height. *Relax,* Adam told himself. *Cushion it.* He raised his foot and met the ball.

It dropped right in front of him. Surprised, he hesitated for a moment.

"Go!" shouted Rodrigo behind him.

Adam sprinted toward the goal on a breakaway. The goalkeeper moved out, trying to cover more of the net. Adam saw the goal, big and wide, gaping on either side of him. He swung his right foot at the ball.

Crunch! A player crashed into Adam's left shoulder, sending him sprawling. He scrambled to his feet, his face caked in mud. The ball bounced away over the goal line, wide of the net.

Tyler stood over him.

"Penalty!" shouted Rodrigo, arms in the air. "Coach — that was a foul."

"No way," called out Coach McKay. "Tyler got the ball. And it was shoulder to shoulder. Corner kick for Blues."

Rodrigo passed Adam as he jogged off to take the corner. "Hey, big, tough hockey guy," he hissed. "Don't let him push you around."

"What do I do on a corner kick?" asked Adam.

Rodrigo pointed at the front of the net. "Just get in

there and find a way to get the ball into the goal!'"

In the penalty area, Adam felt a firm tug on the back of his shirt. He cut left quickly and felt another tug. He looked back. Tyler was covering him, very closely.

As the ball left Rodrigo's foot, Adam remembered a power-play goal he'd once scored in hockey.

He leaned into Tyler. The boy pushed back. But as he did, Adam moved out of the way.

Tyler stumbled and fell.

Adam saw the ball clear the goalkeeper. He jumped, hurling himself at the ball. Just before it reached his head, he closed his eyes.

His whole face exploded with pain. He felt a warm trickle of blood running out of his nose. He tasted its saltiness on his tongue.

"What a header!" someone hollered.

Adam wiped his watering eyes once, then wiped them again. He looked up. The ball was resting in the back of the net.

"Yes!" he burst out, pumping his fist.

"Great goal!" shouted Jit, jogging over and high-fiving him.

Rodrigo wrapped an arm around Adam's shoulders. "Nice header," he laughed. "That just might be the hardest I've ever seen anyone hit a ball with their face."

9 BLACK EYE

"Adam! What on earth happened to your eye?"

Adam's mother closed the front door behind her. She put her bag down on the couch.

"He got hit by a girl," said Jonah, then collapsed into fits of laughter.

Adam didn't even look away from the hockey video game they had been playing.

"Get a life, Jonah," he said. "He's right, though, Mom. In gym class today, playing soccer, I slipped and ran into some girl's elbow."

She looked at him. "Hmm," she said. "I think that face of yours could use some disinfectant and then some ice."

"Mom — I'm fine," groaned Adam.

"It'll only take a few minutes. C'mon — let's get you cleaned up."

Adam paused his game. He followed her to the kitchen.

She pointed to a chair. "Sit and lean back," she said.

She wiped Adam's face carefully. He felt the sting of the disinfectant against a cut on his nose.

"There," said his mother, throwing away the red-streaked tissues. She brought a bag of frozen peas from the freezer. "Hold this against your eye."

The cold peas dulled the pain around Adam's nose and left eye.

"So," said his mother, sitting down next to him, "are you gonna tell me what really happened?"

Adam lowered the bag of peas and looked at her, confused. "What do you mean?"

"This didn't happen in gym class, did it?"

Adam felt panic rising in his chest. Did his mother somehow know about the soccer team? If she did, she would surely tell his father. Adam didn't think he could handle that.

"Did you get in a fight?" she asked.

"A fight?" Adam blurted out, surprised by the question. "No, no, no, Mom." He touched his nose gingerly. "Actually, to tell you the truth, I was kicking around a ball with Rodrigo and I tried a header. I kinda messed it up."

For the hundredth time since practice, Adam saw the ball soaring off Rodrigo's boot. Then he saw the ball lying cradled in the back of the net. His nose throbbed — it was a glorious pain.

"So why didn't you just tell the truth?" asked his mother.

"I dunno," said Adam, avoiding her eyes. "You know what Dad's like about soccer. I was worried you'd tell him."

"You know what, Adam?" said his mother, placing her hand on his arm. "You're allowed to do what makes you happy. If you enjoy kicking a soccer ball around with Rodrigo, you shouldn't feel ashamed of it."

Deep down, Adam knew his mother was right. But he just couldn't quite bring himself to tell her about the team.

His thoughts flashed back to the soccer field. Jit high-fiving him after the goal. Rodrigo's arm around his shoulders. Nobu the keeper clapping his padded gloves together.

The final team list would be on the school website at seven-thirty, Coach McKay had said. Adam glanced at the clock. It was six-thirty.

I have to make this team, thought Adam. *I have to.*

Jonah clomped into the kitchen. "Hey, idiot, are we playing today or what?" he said to Adam.

"Watch it, mouthy boy," warned their mother. "It's dinnertime, anyway."

Adam's father had phoned from the office to say that he'd be late, so they started without him. When Adam saw that dinner was chili and Caesar salad, his stomach growled. He dived into his meal with gusto.

Jonah sat there trolling his spoon in slow circles. He hated chili.

"Can I have some more, Mom?" asked Adam, handing over his empty bowl.

The front door of the house banged open and shut. Adam's father breezed into the room.

"Hey guys!" he exclaimed. "Mmm, chili — your favourite, eh, Jonah?"

He laughed and ruffled his younger son's hair.

"Good day, hon?" asked their mother.

"Very busy," replied their father. He leaned over and kissed her on the cheek. "But not too bad, I suppose."

Adam's father sat down. He looked at Adam.

"What in the world happened to your face, bud?" he exclaimed.

"Got hit by a girl," said Jonah. He laughed and some chili spilled from his mouth onto the floor.

"A girl?" said Adam's father, chuckling. "Have you been playing the field already, Adam?"

"Aw, Dad . . ." said Adam. He never knew what to say when his father made jokes about girlfriends and dating and that kind of stuff. It made him want to crawl into a hole and hide.

"It was just an accident in gym class," said Adam, shrugging. He tried to look his father in the eye as he spoke, but couldn't.

"Oh, right — your *soccer* class," groaned his father. "Only in that dumb sport would they have you playing with girls at your age. Unbelievable."

Adam wasn't sure whether he was supposed to reply or not.

"Your turn to do the dishes, Adam," said his mother.

"Jonah, why don't you go do some homework or something in your room?"

"Can I borrow your laptop, Dad?" asked Jonah.

"Sure, bud," said his father.

Adam rushed through the dishes as quickly as possible. He couldn't stop looking at the clock.

The numbers changed. *Seven-thirty*. Adam's heart raced. The team list would be up.

On his way to Jonah's bedroom to get the laptop, he passed his parents' bedroom.

"So what are you trying to say?" he heard his father ask, sounding offended. "Because it sounds like you're saying I don't want the best for our son."

"That's not it at all," said Adam's mother. "I just wish you would be a bit more careful with what you say to Adam. He's still having trouble finding his place in Vancouver, you know — just like anyone would after such a big change."

"You think I don't know that?" said Adam's father. "I feel guilty every day when I think about taking him away from Jason and all his other Castlegar friends. Has Adam mentioned any of the guys from the Elite League tryouts, by the way? I was hoping he'd make friends on the team."

"No." Adam's mother paused for a moment. "He only talks about Rodrigo. You know, Rodrigo has been friends with Adam since his first day at school."

"That little foreign kid —" snorted Adam's father.

Don't say anything about soccer, Mom, thought Adam. *Please, please don't.*

"Don't give me that look," said his father now. "You think I'm being racist or small-minded or something —"

"Well, aren't you?" said Adam's mother firmly.

There was silence for a moment.

"No, of course not," Adam heard his father say. "I just worry about Adam getting . . . you know, confused about what's important if he has the wrong friends."

"The wrong friends — what does that even mean? Shouldn't Adam be able to decide what's important to him and who he wants to be friends with?"

"Of course," said his father. "I just don't want him to miss opportunities and regret it later."

Adam heard footsteps coming toward the door. He quickly ducked into Jonah's bedroom.

Jonah was sitting on his bed, watching a video of Canucks goalie Roberto Luongo on the computer. Loud music blared from the speakers.

"Awesome!" Jonah exclaimed, as Luongo made a big glove save. He mimed the action, swinging his arm around. Then he slumped back onto his bed.

"Do you think I'll ever get to play in goal?" he asked Adam.

"You know what Dad thinks about that," said Adam, feeling a little sorry for his brother. "And I really don't think tonight's the best night to ask him."

Adam sat staring at the screen, his thoughts swirling.

I'm the reason my parents are arguing again, he thought. His heart sank.

Mom always listens to me, he thought. *But Dad's my biggest fan. He never misses a game or practice. I can't let him down.*

But why did his father have a problem with Rodrigo? And why, really, with soccer?

There was a knock and Adam's father pushed the door open. "Hey Jonah," he said tiredly. "Time for sleep, bud. Go brush your teeth."

Adam dragged himself off Jonah's bed.

"And I'm sorry, Adam," said his father. "But I kind of need that laptop. I've got some work to do for tomorrow. You don't need it for schoolwork, do you?"

"No." Adam handed the laptop to his father and headed for his room.

The team! he thought, as he sank down on his bed, heart thumping. *Did I make it or not?*

He heard the phone ring. Adam's father appeared in the doorway. "It's for you, Adam." He raised one eyebrow. "Rogerino."

Adam took the phone and half-whispered, "Hey, Rodrigo, hang on a minute." He watched his father leave, then stood up and closed his bedroom door. "Okay, what?"

Adam felt so nervous that he thought he might actually throw up.

"Can you believe it?" hollered Rodrigo. "In your

first year ever playing soccer! You are now a Point Grey Dragon!"

Adam felt like opening his window and shouting at the top of his lungs. "I made it?" he said, sitting down slowly. "Really?"

"You mean you haven't looked? We both made it!" exclaimed Rodrigo.

"Couldn't, my dad's computer was ..." Adam began, but he heard his father in the hallway. "Never mind. Gotta go. Talk to you tomorrow."

Adam stood up. He stared into the mirror next to his Sidney Crosby poster. His black eye stared back at him proudly, like a badge of membership.

He'd made the team. He belonged to the team. And no one was going to take that team away.

10 TYLER'S TACKLE

"Man, your boots stink!" declared Rodrigo, turning away.

Adam pulled his dirt-covered boots out of his locker. "Yeah, the girl next to me never stops complaining." He grinned.

"They've been in there the whole week?" asked Rodrigo, holding his nose.

"Yup," said Adam, shrugging. "Can't keep them at home. Hey, when's your dad back again?"

"Saturday night," said Rodrigo. "We can do the work on Sunday morning."

"Damn," said Adam. "I was hoping to get that stick before my next hockey practice."

"When's the practice?" asked Rodrigo.

"Saturday at one."

"What?" exclaimed Rodrigo, eyes wide. "But our first soccer game's Saturday at noon!"

Adam slammed his locker shut. "You can't be serious! What am I gonna do?"

"Well, your hockey's just a practice, right?" replied Rodrigo.

"It's a tryout," said Adam, shaking his head. They walked toward the stairway.

"But this game's a big one — a cup match all the way out in Richmond. You can't miss it!"

Adam knew his friend was right. He'd actually made the soccer team. How could he miss the first game?

Adam pictured his father's face. He tried to push it out of his mind, but couldn't.

After school, practice started with a light warm-up, followed by some sprints.

"Well done, Burnett," shouted Coach McKay as Adam raced to the last cone. "All right, everyone in for a moment."

The players gathered around.

"Our first competition this year," said the coach, "is the Greater Vancouver Cup. Each round is two games against the same team. The scores are added together to determine the winner."

"Our first opponent," he went on, "is Richmond High. They're one of the strongest teams in the whole province. Last year, they thrashed us 5–0."

"We'll get 'em this year, though, Coach," said Jit. Shouts and cheers erupted from the whole team until Coach McKay shushed them. Adam looked around. It was really exciting to see everyone so enthusiastic about the game. He could almost forget that they played soccer together, instead of hockey.

I'm so glad I made this team, he thought.

"It's gonna be tough, boys," said Coach McKay. "So treat training today like a real game. No half-efforts."

"C'mon, guys!" shouted Jit.

The team divided up into Red Bibs and Blue Bibs as usual.

Coach McKay blew the whistle.

"Let's do this!" Adam shouted to his teammates.

Rodrigo passed the ball to Adam, who cushioned it with his left foot. Adam saw Tyler rush toward him and prepared to pass the ball.

Shield the puck, his father always said. *You always rush things.*

Adam swivelled, protecting the ball with his body. All Tyler could do was lean against him, then try a sliding tackle. Adam pushed the ball in the other direction, leaving Tyler sprawled on the ground.

"Adam!" shouted Rodrigo, waving at him.

Adam knocked the ball long. Rodrigo skipped past one defender, then another, and pushed the ball wide.

Adam raced into the middle.

"Cross it!" he shouted.

Rodrigo sent a low, hard pass skimming across the turf.

Adam hit the ball with his right foot. His shot nearly took the goalkeeper's head off on its way into the net.

"Yes!" Adam pumped his fist.

Rodrigo ran across and high-fived him. So did the rest of the Blue Bibs.

"Great pass, Rodrigo — nice finish, Adam," said Jit. "Let's keep it going, guys."

The game continued. Adam watched, amazed, as Rodrigo controlled a long pass. The ball seemed to stick to his friend like a magnet.

There was a corner kick for the Red Bibs. Their speedy little striker curled the ball into the goal area. Blues goalkeeper Nobu jumped up and caught it cleanly.

"Nobu!" shouted Rodrigo, sprinting upfield.

A quick throw from Nobu landed at Rodrigo's feet. Tyler rushed to close him down. The smaller boy feinted left with his head, then nipped the ball through Tyler's legs. He sent a looping pass over Adam's head. Just outside the penalty area, the ball bounced.

Adam surged ahead.

"Over here!" yelled Rodrigo to his left.

Adam's pass wasn't great — it bounced wildly toward his friend. But somehow Rodrigo swivelled and managed to smash the ball right out of mid-air. A pair of defenders closed on him like a pair of scissors. He tumbled to the turf. The ball flew into the top corner of the net.

"What a goal!" someone shouted.

"You'll never score one like that again in this lifetime, Rodrigo," hollered Coach McKay. "Right in the top corner!"

Adam caught Tyler glaring at Rodrigo.

A Blue Bibs defender tackled a Red Bibs player. He passed the ball to Rodrigo. Once again Tyler tried to close him down. Once again Rodrigo slipped the ball past him, then hoofed the ball forward.

Suddenly there was a sickening crunch and a cry of pain from Rodrigo.

Adam spun around. His friend was lying on the ground, clutching his leg. Next to him, Tyler was clambering to his feet.

"I'm s-s-sorry," he stammered, backing away slowly.

Adam sprinted over and shoved Tyler hard in the chest. "Hey!" he burst out angrily. "What do you think you're doing?"

Tyler didn't argue. He just stared at Rodrigo on the ground.

"He's your teammate!" said Adam. He grabbed the front of Tyler's shirt. "And we've got a game Saturday. He's our best player!"

Adam was about to throw a punch, but Jit grabbed his arm. "Back off, man," he shouted, pulling Adam away. Adam pushed back at Jit, blood boiling.

"C'mon, dude," said Jit. "Let it go. Just let it go."

Adam looked over at Tyler.

"Give Rodrigo some space," growled Coach McKay. He turned to Tyler. "Barthson — you stand over there!" He pointed at Adam. "Burnett — over there."

Red-faced, Coach McKay kneeled to help Rodrigo

up. The quick little midfielder limped slowly to the sideline, leaning hard on the coach's arm.

Adam clenched his fists.

Jit spun on Tyler. "What the hell is wrong with you?" he demanded.

Tyler shook his head. "I don't know," he said. "He was just getting by me every time, making me look like an idiot. I was worried I'd lose my place on the team."

"But, Tyler, you're our best central midfielder!" exclaimed Jit. "I asked Coach McKay to play you against Rodrigo so that you'd be prepared for Richmond. You and Rodrigo are on the same side!"

Coach McKay returned. "I think he's okay," he said. "Practice is over for today, gentleman." He pointed at Tyler. "Barthson, follow me."

Tyler followed the coach, his head in his hands.

"Burnett, Dherari — take Rodrigo to see the nurse," said Coach McKay.

Still furious, Adam followed Jit to where Rodrigo was on the sideline.

"I could kill that guy," said Adam. "Honestly. What an idiot."

Jit shook his head. "At the moment, so could I. But Tyler's been my friend since elementary school. He's got a temper, but he's never done anything like this before. And he's a good player — he just loses confidence sometimes."

"None of that helps Rodrigo much now," said Adam.

"I know," said Jit. "I'm just saying."

They reached the sideline.

"You all right there, Rodrigo?" asked Jit.

"Ah . . . yeah," said Rodrigo, hobbling and wincing. "Just a bruise, I think. Didn't twist it."

Jit and Adam hooked Rodrigo's arms over their shoulders. Then they helped their injured teammate up the stairs into the school.

★★★

"You're doing *what* on Saturday?" bellowed Adam's father later that evening. He slammed down his glass so hard that the table shook.

"Look, Dad, I'm sorry," Adam tried to explain. "It's for science class — a marine biology trip. We're going to the docks out in Steveston to learn about commercial fishing. It's for school. It's not like I want to go!"

"Un-*bloody*-believable," said Adam's father. "You can't miss the last Elite League tryout!"

He turned to Adam's mother. "Back me up on this," he said.

"It's a school thing," said Adam's mother, shrugging. "What can we do?" She shot a questioning look at Adam.

Adam's father sat still, his lips pressed hard together. Adam winced, bracing for a flood of angry words.

Instead, his father simply stood up. "Okay," he said.

"You're right, school is maybe the only thing more important than hockey. I'm sure the coach will understand. Adam was absolutely awesome at that first tryout."

"Thanks, Dad," said Adam, nodding. He walked slowly out of the room.

He felt sick to his stomach. So many lies to his father — he hadn't wanted it to be like this.

Maybe I should just play hockey, he considered.

But then he thought of Rodrigo and Jit and Nobu — and even Tyler.

It wasn't that he didn't want to challenge himself in the Elite League. It wasn't even that he suddenly liked soccer better than hockey. It was just that right now the Dragons were the team that mattered to him the most.

Maybe it'll be okay, he told himself. *Maybe I can play on the Elite team and play soccer and just never tell him.*

But deep down, he knew that the only way he could keep playing soccer would be to quit the Elite League.

He just couldn't quite bring himself to say it, even to himself.

11 ADAM'S FIRST GAME

"I knew you'd come!" exclaimed Rodrigo. He crossed the Point Grey parking lot limping, but only slightly. He gave Adam a high-five.

The bus got to Richmond High just after eleven. Sitting in the changing room, Adam pulled on his red shirt with the number 7 on the back, white shorts, and red socks. He looked down at his hands. They were shaking.

The team warmed up next to a big field where a senior boys' match was taking place. Adam felt a ball smack into his shin pad.

"Come on, Adam — focus!" called Rodrigo. "That was right on your foot!"

Swearing at himself, Adam ran after the ball.

He sent a long pass back to Rodrigo. It flew over his friend's head. He swore again and kicked the grass in front of him.

"Take it easy," said Rodrigo. As the game on the field finished, he ran past and gave his friend a whack on the back. "C'mon, we can do this!" Then he added, "Hey, let's go. Coach McKay's calling everyone in."

"Team," said Coach McKay when they had all gathered around him. "Tyler wants to say something."

Tyler stood in front of his teammates. "Guys," he said, "I just want to say that I'm sorry. To the team, and especially to Rodrigo. I put my own feelings ahead of the team. I'd do anything to go back and change it."

"Okay," said Coach McKay to everyone. "This is not my team. It's yours. So it's up to you whether he plays or not."

Rodrigo spoke up. "I say let him play, Coach. Everyone makes mistakes. And we might need someone tough like Tyler out there today."

"I agree," said someone else.

"All in favour?" asked the coach.

Fifteen hands went up. Slowly, Adam raised his hand too.

He looked at Tyler's face and was surprised at what he saw there. For a moment Adam thought Tyler might actually cry with joy.

"Listen up," said Coach McKay. "You already know the starting lineup. There's just one change."

A murmur ran through the players.

"Simon's knee is giving him trouble," said Coach McKay, pointing to their small speedy striker. "So Adam Burnett will be starting up front. You ready, Burnett?"

There was an explosion of clapping all around

Adam. Several players patted him on the back. "C'mon Adam!" someone shouted.

Adam's own knees felt like they might collapse. *First soccer game of my life,* he thought. *And I'm starting.*

"No problem," he said, trying to sound tough.

"Good," said Coach McKay. "Some of you have played the Richmond Giants before. You know what to expect. They are always physical, especially big Number 10, their central defender. Don't back down, but don't let him get to you either. And their speedy danger man up front is Number 5. Remember what he did to us last year — four goals. Don't take your eye off him for a second."

"Let's get this first game, guys," he continued. "Go, Dragons!"

"Go, Dragons!" echoed the players.

The teams jogged onto the field. At centre, a coin was flipped. The referee's whistle sounded.

It was all a blur to Adam until the ball landed at his feet. *I'm in a real soccer game*, he realized. The thought thudded into him like the toughest of bodychecks.

"Adam!" called someone. Adam kicked the ball blindly. A body slammed into his shoulder, knocking him to the ground.

Adam jumped to his feet. His opponent was already jogging away. He was a tall, muscular boy with long, wavy dark hair. He had a white 10 on the back of his blue-and-gold jersey.

Upfield, Rodrigo was trying to find a way past a gigantic Richmond defender. Adam watched his friend feint left and go right. But the big defender swung his leg like an axe, chopping Rodrigo down.

"Ref!" shouted Coach McKay furiously. But no whistle came.

The big defender lumbered upfield. He dipped his shoulder and beat one man. He pushed past another. Then he sent the ball toward Richmond's speedy Number 5, who was sprinting for the Point Grey goal.

Crunch! Tyler slid in, sending Number 5 and the ball flying.

Faking a pass to his right, Tyler side-footed the ball to Jit. Looking up, Jit hit the ball long.

Adam jumped as high as he could. The ball skimmed off the top of his head.

He spun around. Rodrigo had sprinted behind him and snagged the ball. Adam followed his friend, legs pumping.

Rodrigo looked up and saw him. But before he could pass the ball, Richmond's Number 10 sliced him to the ground.

The referee waved them to play on.

The first half continued, a messy midfield battle of rough tackles, free kicks, and misplaced passes. With halftime fast approaching, there still hadn't even been a shot on goal.

"Hold the ball!" shouted Tyler, passing to Adam.

Unable to turn, Adam leaned back against a fierce Richmond defender.

"Adam!" called Jit, running toward him.

Adam passed but he was off-balance. The ball zoomed past Jit's despairing lunge. A speedy Richmond midfielder nicked it and zipped down the right sideline. With a lightning-quick cross, he caught the Point Grey defenders napping.

Richmond's Number 5 met the ball with his right boot. It flew past Nobu into the bottom right corner of the goal. Cheering Richmond players mobbed their striker in a swarm of gold and blue.

As soon as the game restarted, the referee blew his whistle for halftime.

Adam swore loudly and punched his fist into his hand.

"Hey," said Rodrigo. "It's only 1–0. We've still got forty minutes to get them back."

After the players drank some water, Jit spoke up, his voice firm but calm. "Guys, do you want this game or what? Those Richmond guys are completely outmuscling us. We've got to be stronger on the ball, or move it quicker."

A whistle blast beckoned the teams back onto the field. Adam found himself jogging alongside Tyler.

"Hey," said Tyler quietly. "Thanks for voting me back onto the team, after what I did to Rodrigo."

Adam thought back to Tyler's tough tackles in the

first half. He'd worked harder than anyone else. "Don't worry about it, man," he said. "Let's get these guys in the second half."

Tyler made a fist and nodded.

Right after the kickoff, the Richmond goalkeeper collected a loose ball. He tried to throw it to one of his defenders. Rodrigo zipped in and intercepted. Feet dancing, he skipped around two vicious tackles and unleashed a clever bending shot.

It clanged off the outside of the post and bounced out for a goal kick. Adam and his teammates groaned. So close!

The Dragons pressed harder. Two more of Rodrigo's shots were saved by the Richmond goalkeeper. Adam smashed a right-footed drive that was blocked by a sliding defender.

"Keep going, guys!" shouted Rodrigo. "We've got them on the run!"

Sprinting forward, Rodrigo intercepted a pass at the top of the Richmond penalty area. He pushed the ball between the last two defenders.

He's in! thought Adam, sprinting after his friend. *This is it!*

But as Rodrigo slipped between them, the defenders lunged. Rodrigo crashed to the turf.

This time the referee's whistle blasted loud and clear.

"Penalty!" shouted people all around.

Adam's first thoughts were of the penalty box in

Castlegar arena. He'd spent a lot of time there. But when the referee pointed to the white dot in the middle of the penalty area, it hit him.

Penalty shot!

And then he saw Rodrigo. Adam's friend was lying on the ground, groaning and clutching the same leg he'd hurt in training.

"C'mon, bud," said Adam anxiously, offering him a hand. "Enough drama stuff. We got the penalty shot."

But Rodrigo closed his eyes tight and pointed to his ankle.

"Coach!" called Adam. "Rodrigo's hurt!"

Coach McKay sprinted across the field. He removed Rodrigo's boot and examined his ankle.

"Sorry, son," he said. "You're done for today."

"I can play!" said Rodrigo. "Just give me a minute."

Coach McKay shook his head. He helped Rodrigo off the field. A tall, lanky player called Laszlo came on as a substitute.

"Adam," shouted the coach. "You take it!"

Me? thought Adam, not believing his ears.

He picked up the ball and placed it on the spot.

Look how close this is, he tried to tell himself. *Nice and easy.*

Leaning forward, he looked at the top right-hand corner of the net. And smashed the ball into it. He raised his arms in triumph.

Twee! sounded the whistle. *Twee!*

"Retake!" snapped the referee. "I didn't signal for you to shoot yet."

Adam was surprised, but he lined the ball up on the spot again. *No problem*, he thought.

He jogged forward. But this time he looked at the goalkeeper and then took the shot.

Clang! The ball struck the crossbar with such force that it flew right back over Adam's head.

He spun around. Richmond was on the counter-attack!

A speedy Richmond midfielder tried to loft a long shot at Nobu. The alert Point Grey goalkeeper back-pedalled and tipped the ball over the crossbar.

"Get back in the box, Adam!" called Jit, pointing at Richmond's big Number 10. "Mark the big guy."

The corner kick curled into the penalty area toward the near post, where Adam was standing. He leaped to head it away. But as he jumped, he felt someone tug the back of his shirt, trying to reach the ball first.

Distracted, Adam took his eye off the ball and it skimmed off the top of his head. He tumbled to the ground.

Cheers erupted all around from the Richmond players. Adam didn't need to look. He knew what had happened.

There, tucked into a corner of the goal, was the ball.

Adam Burnett had scored in his first real soccer game — on the wrong net!

12 THE BOOTS UNDER THE BED

Adam opened his eyes. On the far wall of his bedroom was his poster of Sidney Crosby. He remembered the soccer stars all over Rodrigo's walls.

Instantly, his thoughts flashed back to the game against Richmond, the game the Dragons had lost 2–0.

Clang! The ball hit the crossbar. *Clang, clang, clang!*

I let the guys down, he told himself. *Both goals were my fault.*

"Adam, you awake?" Adam's father pushed the door open, and smiled. "Hey, bud," he said. "Must've been quite the field trip. Your mom says you've been snoring for three hours."

"Yeah, I guess I —" Adam yawned loudly "— fell asleep."

"Listen, Adam, about hockey today," said his father calmly. "Well, I called Coach Wilson and —"

Suddenly something half under the bed caught his father's eye.

"What in the world?" he exclaimed.

Oh crap, thought Adam. There on the floor were his dirt-encrusted soccer boots. He'd planned to hide them, then take them back to school. But he'd been so angry about the missed penalty and scoring on his own net that he'd just thrown his bag on the floor and crashed into bed.

Adam's father picked up a boot. He examined it like it was some sort of diseased animal. "Where'd you get these?" he demanded.

"R-Rodrigo," Adam sputtered. "He loaned them to me. For PE."

His father's eyes narrowed. "What's that under your sweatshirt, Adam?"

"Nothing . . ." began Adam, but it was too late. He remembered. He hadn't taken off his soccer jersey yet.

"Adam, *what* is under your sweatshirt?" repeated his father, pointing.

Reluctantly, Adam pulled off his black Castlegar Hockey hoodie. His Dragons uniform shone bright red in the sunlight coming through his bedroom window.

Adam's father stared at the jersey, then at the boot in his hand. He looked at Adam.

"There was no field trip today," he said, looking dazed.

Adam's mother appeared in the doorway, smiling. "Hey, is Lazybones up yet or . . ."

She stopped. "What's going on?" she asked. She glanced from Adam to his father and back again.

"Our son," said Adam's father, holding up the soccer

boot and shaking his head, "has been misleading us. It seems he has decided he's a *soccer* player."

He turned to Adam. "I can't believe you lied about this."

Adam felt a lump in his throat. Before he could stop them, tears started to form in his eyes.

Adam's mother broke in. "And what did you expect him to do? You never listen to Adam. You never ask him what he wants. So what if he wants to play soccer or hockey or tic-tac-toe?"

"Did you know about this?" asked Adam's father in disbelief.

"Not about the team," she replied. "I thought he was just kicking around a ball with Rodrigo in the park."

"It all makes sense," groaned Adam's father. "That's who put this crazy soccer idea into Adam's head — that little Mexican kid."

"Rodrigo's from Uruguay, Dad," said Adam, forcing himself to speak. "And it's not his fault. He was the only person who was nice to me when school started."

"Why can't you be glad that Adam's made a friend?" demanded Adam's mother. "It doesn't matter that he's from a different country."

"But Dad's right, Mom," Adam added. "The soccer was a crazy idea. I was terrible today in the game." He thought of Rodrigo and Jit and his other teammates, and how he'd let them down.

They'll be better off without me, he thought. Tears filled his eyes again.

"Look, Adam," said his father firmly. "I know moving here hasn't been easy for any of us. But sneaking around, hiding things, telling lies — we can't have that in this family. I'm afraid we'll have to ground you."

Adam thought of the stick money. Weren't he and his father hiding that from his mother? It all seemed so unfair.

"I think," said Adam's mother to his father, "that Adam's been under a lot of stress recently. How about no grounding this time, and we all agree to be more honest with one another from now on?"

Adam's father opened his mouth to argue, but stopped himself. "Well, I guess so," he said. "But it had better not happen again, Adam."

Adam looked at his father and nodded slowly.

"Good, I'm glad that's understood." His father moved toward the door, but turned back before leaving the room. "Oh, and I spoke to Coach Wilson this afternoon," he said. "Because you are a talented player, he said he'd give you one more chance. You're very lucky."

After his father had left the room, Adam turned to his mother.

"Mom," he said, wiping his eyes. "I'm sorry I lied."

His mother walked over and sat down next to him.

"Adam —" she put an arm around his shoulder "— do you like soccer?"

"I said I'm no good at it."

"Yeah," she said. "I heard you. But I asked if you like it."

"I don't know," said Adam. "I didn't know anyone here at first. Rodrigo was the only person who talked to me at school. So when he suggested soccer, I just kinda went for it. And yeah — I was surprised how much I liked it. And the other guys on the team were getting to like me too — at least until I lost the game for them.

"At the first Elite League tryout," he went on, "everyone was so mean and unfriendly to each other. It just made me miss my friends back in Castlegar."

"What if," said his mother, "there was a way to play hockey and soccer?"

"But wouldn't I have to give up the Elite League?" said Adam.

"Well, yes. If you want to play soccer," she said, "that would be the only way. But you could still play house hockey."

Adam looked down at the Dragons shirt he was still wearing. He didn't want to give it up and lose his teammates.

But Adam couldn't forget the look on his father's face after seeing that bright red jersey and the boots half-hidden under the bed.

★★★

"Oof!" exclaimed Rodrigo. "I can't believe Dad makes me do this kinda stuff. He could easily afford a gardener." He lifted a heavy shovelful of dark soil and walked over to the big pile of dirt they'd made.

He claimed his ankle was all better. Adam thought he was still limping a bit.

Adam stuck his shovel into the soft ground. He pried out a chunk of grass and dirt. "Never mind," he said. "Almost done."

"Man, I can't wait until Wednesday!" exclaimed Rodrigo. He hadn't stopped talking about the next Richmond game all morning.

"Mmm," mumbled Adam, avoiding Rodrigo's eyes. He still hadn't told his friend that he didn't think he could play soccer anymore.

Adam pushed the wheelbarrow over to the big dirt pile. He dumped it and Rodrigo spread the dirt around with a hoe.

"We just have to plant these now," Rodrigo said, pointing to a box full of small plants.

Adam scooped out the soil to make three rows of little holes. Rodrigo put in the plants and packed soil around them.

"*Muy bueno!*" shouted a voice behind him. It was Rodrigo's father, giving them two thumbs up. He walked down the front steps of the house and out onto the lawn.

"My new and so much beautiful garden." His accent was much thicker than Rodrigo's.

He handed the boys eighty dollars each. "Your pay, gentlemen."

"Thank you so much, sir," said Adam, taking the four $20 bills between his grubby fingers.

Rodrigo folded his money and put it in his pocket.

"So, Adam," said Rodrigo's father. "I hear you two has very big soccer match this Wednesday. First game no go so well, I hear?"

"Don't worry, Dad," said Rodrigo. "We're gonna beat them this time, eh, Adam?"

"My boy — already so very Canadian. He say 'eh' a lot and many other words I don't know. Because in Uruguay your English teacher a Canadian fellow, no?" laughed Rodrigo's father. He nudged his son. "No bad words, I hope.

"Anyway," he added, walking back toward the house, "see you Wednesday, Adam. I want to see goals, goals, goals."

"Dude," said Adam after Rodrigo's father was gone. "I'm sorry but — I just can't play on Wednesday."

"*What?*" shouted Rodrigo. "But it's the cup! If we lose, we're eliminated!"

"I know, I know," said Adam. "But after tomorrow, I'm gonna have hockey pretty much every day."

"But the Dragons need you!" exclaimed Rodrigo.

"Aw, c'mon," said Adam, turning away. "You saw me last game — I'm no soccer player."

"You've got size, speed, and strength," pleaded

Rodrigo. "Three things I would kill to have. You just had a couple of bad bounces!"

Adam didn't know what to say. "Look, I've — I've got to go," he stammered. He turned to walk away.

"Hey man," called Rodrigo after him, "I know you're not a quitter. Why don't you have the guts to try again?"

Adam didn't look back. He walked quickly home, his thoughts spinning out of control.

I'm going to lose the one friend I have here, he thought miserably. All around him, the city seemed huge, empty, uncaring.

When Adam got home, he saw his father sitting in the living room reading a magazine. Knowing that his hands were still dirty from gardening, he kept them in his pockets.

"Hi, Dad," Adam said as he walked by. "Can I please borrow your laptop?"

"What for?" asked his father.

"I want to send an email to Jason and the Castlegar guys," he answered truthfully.

Maybe no one in Vancouver cares what I think, thought Adam. *But those guys always do.*

"No problem, bud," said his father. "It's on the kitchen table, I think."

Adam washed his hands, then took the laptop up to his room. He set it up on his bed and signed in. But before he could start writing to Jason and Graham, messages started popping up on his screen.

Nobu Roppongi: ADAM, UR BIG HEAD IS MY TARGET FOR GOALKICKS! WE NEED U!

Jit Dherari: WE CAN'T BEAT RICHMOND WITHOUT U!

Tyler Barthson: WE'RE NOT TOUGH ENOUGH WITHOUT U, BIG GUY!

Rodrigo Davila: HEY ICE MAN. THIS IS YOUR GAME.

Adam stared at the screen in disbelief. Messages kept popping up.

This is my team, he thought. *These guys are my friends.*

Adam finally knew what he had to do. He stood up and walked to the living room. Facing his father, he took sixty of the eighty dollars he'd earned at Rodrigo's out of one pocket. Then he pulled the other $140 that his father had given him out of the other. "I spent sixty dollars on those soccer boots, Dad," he admitted. "But I worked for Rodrigo's dad to make up for it. Here's the money back," he said, handing the bills to his stunned father.

"What money?"

Adam and his father both looked up in surprise. Adam's mother had slipped into the living room unnoticed.

"What money?" she repeated.

"Well, I — I —" sputtered Adam's father, "I gave Adam a little money for a new stick."

"How much is 'a little'?"

"Two hundred dollars," Adam's father admitted.

"*Two hundred dollars?*" she exclaimed. "But you know money's tight right now and —"

"Okay, okay, so maybe I went a *little* overboard," Adam's father said. "But it's not like we couldn't afford it, really. Especially when it was to help Adam achieve his dreams."

"It's not even the money so much," retorted Adam's mother. "What about being honest with each other? When was I going to know about this?"

"Look," said Adam's father, lowering his voice, "maybe you're right. Maybe I made a mistake. But Adam's given the money back now. And he showed me last hockey practice that he doesn't need a fancy new stick. Can't we just put this behind us?"

Adam took a deep breath, then said, voice shaking, "Dad, the other guys on the Elite team — I don't like them. They just see me as competition."

Adam stopped, unsure if he could really force out the words he needed to say. He tried to look his father in the eye, but couldn't.

"I'd still like to join a house league hockey team again, like the Rebels," he said at last. "But I'm not going to play in the Elite League. I'm going to play soccer for the Point Grey Dragons."

13 STRIKER

Adam got to the changing room on Wednesday before his teammates. He set his bag down on a bench, and pulled out his uniform, boots, and shin pads.

"Hey man — you up for this?" said someone behind him. Adam turned.

It was Tyler. He extended his hand, and Adam took it. "Let's do this," he said.

The rest of the players started showing up. Suddenly the room was full of high-fives and nervous laughter.

Rodrigo sat down next to Adam. "This is gonna be awesome," he said. He clapped Adam on the back. "Glad you're here, man."

Adam was happy to have his teammates around him. It had been a rough couple of days at home. His father hadn't spoken to him since Sunday. And he'd heard his parents having muffled arguments behind closed doors.

Coach McKay walked into the room. "Not much to say, guys," he said. "We've dug ourselves a 2–0 hole. Now it's time to get out."

"Go, Point Grey!" shouted Jit.

"Go, Dragons!" hollered someone else. Players began to leave the room.

"Hey," said Coach McKay, waving Adam over. "Simon is still injured, so you're up front. Hold the ball, use your strength, and look to pass out wide. Don't be afraid to shoot from anywhere."

"And," he added quietly, "you've seen how these guys play. Don't let them push Rodrigo around. He's not a hundred percent today, with that ankle. No hockey fists, of course —" Adam grinned "— but let them know you mean business."

Out on the pitch warming up, Adam caught sight of Rodrigo's father down behind the Richmond goal. He was wearing a large black coat that looked far too warm for September. He waved. Adam waved back.

Adam's thoughts wandered back to his hockey games in Castlegar — his dad in the crowd, cheering him on. For the thousandth time since Sunday, he wondered if his father would ever understand his decision.

"Hey Adam, we're starting," called Rodrigo.

As he jogged to the halfway line, Adam glanced one more time at Rodrigo's father.

He stopped in shock. He couldn't believe his eyes.

His whole family was standing next to Mr. Davila. Adam's mother and Jonah were clapping their hands. Adam's father was staring down at the ground, arms folded. He looked like he wanted to be somewhere else.

A whistle sounded and the ball zipped toward Adam. It bounced away off his shin pad.

Focus! he told himself angrily. He raced after the ball. A tall Richmond midfielder got there just before him. Adam launched into a sliding tackle, sweeping away the ball and the player's legs.

"Great tackle!" shouted Coach McKay.

Jit scooped up the ball and streaked down the left side. He sent a hard pass toward Rodrigo, who was just outside the Richmond penalty area. Rodrigo controlled the ball perfectly on his knee. He swivelled to volley it.

Crunch! An elbow from Richmond's big Number 10 sent Rodrigo sprawling. The referee blew his whistle.

Adam sprinted over. He stuck his finger in the Richmond player's face.

"You'd better watch it," he snarled. Number 10 pretended to laugh as if he didn't care. But he backed away from Adam pretty quickly.

"Back off, Number 7 Red!" shouted the referee at Adam. "Number 10 Blue, come here." He flashed his yellow card at the Richmond defender.

"I've got this," said Rodrigo to Adam, picking up the ball. "Go for the rebound if the goalie stops it."

Adam stood just inside the box. A defender jostled him from the side. Adam glanced quickly at the ref. He wasn't looking. Adam gave the boy a quick little jab with his elbow.

Rodrigo ran in from the side and smashed the ball with his right foot.

Adam watched the ball soar over his head. He spun around, ready to pounce on a rebound. *Nah, that's going way wide*, he thought, relaxing.

The goalkeeper made the same mistake. Rodrigo's shot curled and dipped at the last moment. It clanged off the underside of the crossbar and into the goal.

The Dragons swarmed all over Rodrigo.

"How'd you do that?" someone shouted.

"Goal of the year!"

"Go, Dragons!"

Behind the goal, Rodrigo's father and Adam's mother were cheering wildly. Jonah was pumping his fist in the air.

Beside them, Adam saw his father clapping. Clapping slowly, but still clapping.

Right from the kickoff, Rodrigo nicked the ball again. He passed to Adam. Adam looked up. The Richmond goalkeeper was standing at the edge of his penalty area. *Shoot from anywhere*, Coach McKay had said.

Adam smashed the ball as hard as he could. It flew over the defenders, cleared the goalkeeper and bounced.

Bounced, bounced, bounced . . .

The goalkeeper scrambled back frantically. Just as the ball neared the line, he dived and tipped it around the post. Adam squeezed his eyes shut in disbelief. So close!

"Good try, Adam!" shouted a man's voice in the distance. Adam looked up. Down behind the net, his father was clapping harder now. Clapping like he meant it.

Rodrigo swung the corner kick toward the far post and Adam sprinted under it. The angle was too wide to score from. Adam spotted a red Point Grey shirt and headed the ball back across the goalmouth.

Jit lunged with his right foot. The ball flew into the far corner.

Jit pumped his fist in the air and ran away, cheering madly. Adam and the rest of the Dragons chased after him.

"It's 2–2, guys!" shouted Rodrigo. "Ours to win!"

Point Grey continued their attack. Adam had one shot saved by the goalkeeper. Rodrigo took a shot that missed by inches.

At the halftime whistle, the Richmond players left the field swearing and arguing.

"Great job, guys!" said Coach McKay. "But remember, every team gets their chances. Stay focused out there."

Richmond's quick striker, Number 5, took the ball from the kickoff. He pushed past two midfielders, surging toward the Point Grey defence. He feinted left, then right; beat one defender, then another. Nobu charged from his goal. Number 5 stepped around him.

The goal was wide open.

Adam cringed as the Richmond striker swung his left foot. But Jit came sliding in from nowhere, sending him flying through the air and tumbling to the turf. The ball bounced away, wide of the net.

"Yeah!" yelled Adam. "What a tackle!"

The whistle sounded, loud and long. Jit put his head in his hands. He shouted in disbelief. The referee sprinted forward and pointed at the penalty spot. And then he reached into his back pocket and pulled out a red card.

"No way, ref!" bellowed Coach McKay. "Terrible decision!"

The referee flashed the card. Jit's head sagged. As he marched toward the sideline, Adam ran over and gave him a whack on the shoulder. "That was the worst call I've ever seen," he said. "Great tackle."

"We've *got* to get this game back, Adam," said Jit, his eyes wide.

The referee blew his whistle. Number 5 jogged forward calmly. The ball flew into the corner past Nobu's desperate dive.

With Point Grey down to ten players, Richmond went for their throats. Number 5 took two long shots, which Nobu somehow managed to tip over the bar. And Tyler slid to block a sizzling header that was hurtling toward the bottom right corner.

Nobu sent a long kick upfield. Rodrigo trapped it cleanly. He was bundled to the ground by Richmond's Number 10. There was no whistle.

Adam passed one to Rodrigo. Number 10 went

right through the back of his ankles. Rodrigo got up wincing and limping. No whistle yet again.

"Wake up, Ref!" shouted Coach McKay.

"Quiet, Coach!" the referee snapped back.

Under heavy pressure, Adam knocked a hopeful ball forward. Rodrigo leaped and somehow managed to control it on his chest. He beat one lunging defender, then another. The third one chopped his feet out from under him and the ball bounced loose. Tyler slid in, boot behind the ball. The Richmond player flew right overtop of him.

"Tyler!" yelled Adam, streaking forward.

Tyler's pass reached Adam's feet just inside the Richmond penalty area. The goalkeeper charged. The net gaped wide and open on either side of him.

"Shoot!" hollered someone.

"Adam!" hollered someone else to his left. Instead of shooting, Adam swivelled and slipped the ball sideways. The goalkeeper clattered into Adam's legs. Adam flew into the air and thudded hard onto the turf.

He looked up just in time to see Tyler slip the ball into the open net.

"Great pass!" called Tyler, high-fiving him. "Open goal!"

"Hey, all tied up again, guys!" cried Rodrigo, clapping them both on the back.

"What a goal!" boomed a big voice behind them. "Way to go, Dragons!"

Adam spun around just in time to see his father high-five Mr. Davila, then pump his fist in the air. Adam's mother was cheering and clapping. Jonah was doing some sort of goal dance.

As Adam ran back toward centre, his legs felt suddenly lighter and stronger beneath him.

From the kickoff, Richmond's Number 10 surged through the Dragons' midfield. He slipped the ball through the defence to Number 5, who shot it past Nobu into the net.

The whistle sounded. The flag was up. Offside.

Too close, thought Adam.

"Don't get too excited, Dragons," Adam heard his father shout. "It's only tied. Focus!"

Nobu sent a long kick forward. Rodrigo outjumped his tall opponent and headed it toward Adam. Rodrigo paid a heavy price. Number 10 landed on top of him, driving him into the ground.

Adam saw a defender out of the corner of his eye. He felt a hand grab at the left side of his shirt.

I've got this guy, he thought. Instead of stopping the ball, he let it slip through his legs.

The defender stumbled.

Adam spun: ball in front, defenders close behind. He looked up. He smashed his right foot through the ball. His shot soared past the keeper's reaching hands.

Pong! The ball rebounded off the crossbar and flew through the air back to him. Adam stumbled forward, defenders all around him. The keeper scrambled to his feet and rushed for the ball.

Adam launched himself forward through the air. His forehead crashed into the ball. The keeper plunged right. But he could only watch as the ball flew past his fingertips.

Goal!

A mountain of red and white piled on top of Adam. Everyone was cheering wildly. Adam staggered to his feet, dizzy and hardly able to breathe.

"What a goal!" shouted his teammates.

Seconds later, the game kicked off and the final whistle blew. Adam's world was once again covered in red shirts and wild cheers.

When he finally scrambled to his feet, a pair of strong arms embraced him.

"Great game, bud," said Adam's father, bearhugging him again. "Man oh man. Crunching hits, clever passes, last-minute goals — I never knew this soccer stuff could be so exciting."

14 BACK ON THE ICE

Three weeks later, Adam led his new hockey team, the Kerrisdale Flames, back to the dressing room after their first league game.

He sat down. A stick thwacked his thick shin guard. A gloved hand punched his left shoulder pad.

"Great game, Adam!"

"What a move on that second goal — the goalie flopped like a fish!"

"Hat trick!"

Grinning, Adam lifted off his helmet and dropped it on the change-room floor. He tugged off his jersey and glanced at it for a moment. It was red and black and had a captain's C on the chest.

After a quick shower, Adam found his father up in the stands, sitting next to Rodrigo and Mr. Davila. Mr. Davila was dressed in another huge coat. He also sported gigantic woolly mitts, a thick scarf and a hat with earflaps. He looked like an Arctic explorer.

"Great game, bud!" exclaimed Adam's father.

"Come sit down. Jonah's game is about to start."

"Adam, that was awesome!" said Rodrigo, giving Adam a little shove.

"Yeah," said Adam, "5–3 — not bad, eh? I can't believe that second goal went —"

"Yeah, yeah, yeah," interrupted Rodrigo. "The goals were cool. But what was even cooler was how you punched that guy and only had to sit in the little penalty box for two minutes!"

"Well, actually, I probably shouldn't have —"

"And you smashed that big fat defenceman against the boards! The referee didn't even seem to notice."

A buzzer sounded somewhere above them. Two teams took to the ice: one in blue jerseys, the other in horrible bright orange.

"The vomit-coloured orange guys are Jonah's team," laughed Adam. "I call them the Traffic Cones, 'cause it's easy to skate around them."

Rodrigo burst out laughing.

"Adam," said Adam's father warningly, but chuckled too.

Adam scanned the ice, confused. "Dad, where's Jonah?"

Adam saw a strange little smile creep across his father's face. He followed his dad's eyes as he pointed to the end of the rink. A small goalie was practising falling down and getting up again.

"Really?" said Adam, mouth gaping open. "You gave in?"

"Yeah," said his dad, taking a sip from his coffee. "You're mother's a great lady, you know. She was right when she told me to listen to you two a bit more. Plus," he smiled, "Jonah promised to do the dishes every night for the rest of his life if I bought him goalie equipment. And he said he'd pay better attention at school, even in French class."

Adam was speechless. The soccer game and now this.

"Yeah," said his father, "I've been reading up on goaltending techniques so I can give him some advice. When I have time, of course. You keep giving me all those soccer magazines from Rodrigo — I've spent hours and I still can't keep all the teams straight!"

I underestimated him, thought Adam, looking at his father.

Out on the ice, Adam's little brother snagged a wrist shot with his glove.

Mr. Davila leaned toward Adam's father. "Can you tell me why your son is come so far from goal?" he asked.

"Well, you see, Fernando," said Adam's father, clearing his throat, "this game of hockey is a bit different from your soccer. There's a lot of skill involved, a lot of knowledge you need. Jonah's cutting down the angle there, making it harder for the shooter to score."

"I see," said Mr. Davila, nodding seriously.

"Dad," laughed Adam, "goalkeepers do that in soccer too."

Mr. Davila spoke again. "And can you please explain me," he asked, "why he is now use that paddle as an axe on the back of other boy's legs?'

"Well, he's . . ." began Adam's father. "Wait a minute. Hey Jonah, cut that out!"

"A little barbaric, this sport," said Mr. Davila.

"Ah, it's just a good tough Canadian game," said Adam's father.

"I think it's awesome," said Rodrigo. "I want to learn! Can you teach me, Adam?"

"Rodrigo, I don't know if that is good idea," said his father, shaking his head.

"No problem, man. We'll go skating next week," replied Adam. "Hey, maybe you'll be the first Uruguayan in the NHL."

Rodrigo's face lit up.

"I want to thank you, by the way, Fernando," said Adam's father to Rodrigo's father, "for giving Adam some work to do in your garden."

"*De nada*," said Rodrigo's father. "No problem. My pleasure. I think children these days should do more hard work like this, don't you?"

"Absolutely." Adam's father nodded. "Their generation just doesn't know how to work hard like ours."

Rodrigo nudged Adam and rolled his eyes.

"So, Rodrigo," said Adam's father as they waited for Jonah after his game, "we've got you converted to hockey already, eh? Maybe we need to work a bit harder on your dad." He reached into his coat pocket and pulled out six tickets. "Won them in a raffle at work!"

"Canucks against Flames?" shouted Adam. "Awesome! Is Mom coming too?"

"You bet," replied his father.

"Can we go, Dad?" pleaded Rodrigo. "Please?"

His father thought for a moment, then smiled. "Why not?" he said. "Thank you very much, Bruce — that is very gesture of kindness. How about we take your family out for some Latin American food on the way downtown?"

"Sounds spicy," said Adam's father. "But like you said, why not?"

Chatting away about soccer, hockey, and food, the two men began to walk toward the main exit. Rodrigo and Jonah followed.

Adam stayed behind for a moment. Setting down his hockey bag, he walked over to the glass at the edge of the rink. He squinted. The goals seemed to expand and widen. Where ice had been, green grass sprouted.

Blinking his eyes, Adam looked again. There was nothing but fresh ice, still wet from the Zamboni. The bright lights reflected off its smooth, flat surface. The nets he'd scored on stood rooted to the ice, chest height as always.

"Coming, Adam?" called his father.

"Wake up, Adam!" shouted Jonah.

With a quick glance backward, Adam followed

them through the heavy doors of the arena and out into the bright autumn sun.

MORE SPORTS, MORE ACTION
www.lorimer.ca

CHECK OUT THESE OTHER SOCCER STORIES FROM LORIMER'S SPORTS STORIES SERIES:

Trading Goals
by Trevor Kew

Vicky lives for soccer, and dreams of being on the national team. But when she suddenly has to switch schools, she finds herself on the same team as her fiercest rival, a goalkeeper named Britney — and there's only room for one girl in the net.

Sidelined
by Trevor Kew

Vicky's select soccer team is bound for a tournament in England — the chance of a lifetime! But when a rivalry with her teammate erupts and competition for a guy's interest drives two friends apart, Vicky learns that no one is truly invincible.

Alecia's Challenge
by Sandra Diersch

Getting used to a new school and a new stepfather is bad enough, then suddenly Alecia's best friend quits the soccer team. Alecia only joined the team to be with Anne — she doesn't even *like* soccer — but now her stepdad won't let her quit!

Corner Kick
by Bill Swan

Michael Strike's the most popular guy in school and the most talented soccer player around. But then a new kid from Afghanistan arrives who can show him up on the field, and threatens to steal his spotlight . . .

Falling Star
by Robert Rayner

He's super-talented on the pitch, but lately Edison seems to have lost his nerve. He hesitates and misses shot after shot. Can a ragtag group of soccer misfits show him what the game is really about before it's too late?

Foul Play
by Beverly Scudamore

When her team's chance at winning a tournament is foiled by freshly-dug holes in their practice field, Remy gets suspicious. Is someone trying to sabotage them? She'll bet everything that the captain of the rival team — her ex-best friend — is behind it.

Just for Kicks
by Robert Rayner

Toby's not the greatest or most athletic player on the field, but he sure loves to play. But when new coaches arrive and try to organize the pickup soccer players into a league, it doesn't matter who's friend, foe, or family — it only matters who wins.

Soccer Showdown
by John Danakas

Lizzie's just been named captain of the soccer team — the *boys'* soccer team — but some of her teammates aren't playing nice. Will it be boys vs. girls forever, or can Lizzie think of a way to settle the score, once and for all?

Little's Losers
by Robert Rayner

The Brunswick Valley soccer team isn't just bad — they're terrible. The worst. So awful, in fact, that their coach gives up and quits. No one is more surprised than they are when they make it to the play-offs, but who will coach them now?

Offside!
by Sandra Diersch

Alecia's soccer team has been through a lot this season, but now they're a tight team and a force on the field. Then a tough new player, Lexi, joins mid-season — and her bad attitude seems to be contagious.

Off the Wall
by Camilla Reghelini Rivers

Soccer is the one thing Lizzie Lucas can look forward to when nothing else seems to be going her way. But then her perfect little sister, who outshines her at everything, decides she wants to play too . . . in the same league.

Out of Sight
by Robert Rayner

Lately, the star goalkeeper on Linh-Mai's team has been acting a little strange — missing easy saves, passing to the wrong teammates, not noticing Linh-Mai's new glasses . . . Linh-Mai thinks he might need glasses of his own, but the problem may turn out to be more serious.

Play On
by Sandra Diersch

Alecia's soccer team has made it to the top of the league, and things finally seem to be looking up. But then a vicious piece of gossip and old rivalries threaten to tear her team apart. Can they get it together in time for the finals?

Soccer Star
by Jacqueline Guest

Sam has spent her whole life moving from place to place. But now she feels like she doesn't know who she really is or where she belongs. In order to "find herself," Sam has a habit of signing up for too many activities at once. But can she be a star at everything?

LORIMER

Suspended
by Robert Rayner

There's a new principal at Brunswick Valley School, and the establishment is out to shut down the soccer team. For team captain Shay Sutton, the only way to fight fire is with fire, and he enlists the aid of two high school thugs to help them out.

Trapped
by Michele Martin Bossley

Nothing seems to be going right for Jane's soccer team this season. Then some of the girls' stuff starts going missing. Everyone points the finger at the new girl, but Jane is determined to find the *real* culprit . . . and get her team back on track.